The Sins of My Beretta 2

Written By: Trenae

D1521351

This book is dedicated to my angel Eli. Eazy you were the strongest baby ever and fought a fight that the doctors claimed you would lose from day one. You showed them all that God has the final say so, not man. You taught us all a lesson in patience and faith in the brief period of time that we knew you. You are now free to move around like you couldn't when you were here. You earned your rest and your wings my love, heaven couldn't wait for you.

Rest in Paradise Eli "Eazy" David Hebert

Acknowledgments

I can't believe that I'm at this point again. This is crazy and I am still waiting for someone to pinch me and wake me up from this dream. This is the most humbling experience ever. Had anyone ever told me that I would be an author, I would call their bluff. But here we are on book two. Well let me start by first thanking the most high, this gift, this drive, this need to please my readers; that's all God. I was lost, I didn't know what I wanted to do or where I would end up; I was at my wits end. When God wants you to listen to him and you are distracted then he will remove those distractions and that's just what he did. It took me to have nothing for me to go back to what I knew HIM! This is my purpose, and I will walk in it. My first thanks will always go to God.

To my parents, Trudy, Jonathon and Tarunye (my mommytwo), Thank ya'll for supporting me in whatever decision I made. I said I wanted to write and ya'll reply was let me know when the book comes out. That was the push I needed and I'm not stopping. I hope I make you all proud when it's all said and done. I love ya'll to the moon and back again.

To my siblings, (this list is long but blame all three of my parents), Leonard, Kevin, Malika, Asia, Tarya, Makiya and Jayanma (deep breath) don't let anyone tell you what you can or can't do. No one can put limitations on you but yourself, shoot for the moon and if you miss and land among the stars shoot further. Whatever you do, DON'T GIVE UP! That has never and will never be an option for us. I love ya'll also.

To my family, man again it's way too many to name but I appreciate each of ya'll. We have arguments like every other family but what sets us apart is despite that we are always there for each other no matter the issue. Thanks for the support, the love, the guidance and above all the prayers. I love ya'll.

Next up, my cousin Raquel, I always single her out because she is truly my role model. Beautiful inside and out and since we were younger I've always looked up to her. I remember being young and always crying to run behind her and her friends, mind you she's like 5 years older than me. The rare moments she would say I couldn't go with her, I was running to my Aunt Betty so she had no choice. I wanted to be just like her as a child and when I grew up it didn't change much at all. I still aspire to be like her except it's no longer in comparison to the way she dresses or her age. It's now more like I wanna be successful like her, happy like her and eventually a great role model and mother to someone. Thanks for being my motivation cuz.

My daily support system, my ears, my walls to bounce ideas off, my confidantes; they were my everything in writing part one and nothing has changed. Chrissy, Fantasia, Kalyn, Kelleashia and Kristen even if I said thank you a million times it wouldn't be enough. Ya'll listened without judgement when I cried, when I complained about being tired and even when I had three million ideas to bounce off of ya'll. The words "Let me get a free copy," never left ya'll lips neither and I respect that ya'll supported even when I wanted to send ya'll the free version. Every time I made a post you all shared it, when I forgot to make posts ya'll did. For that I'll be forever grateful for my circle. I love ya'll.

To the ladies of my readers group, Lipstick & Tea With Trenae', thank you for the countless laughs and deep conversations you all provide me with on a daily. I look forward to the group growing and hopefully meeting you ladies from surrounding cities and states.

To my pen sisters at KKP, we are up next! Stay humble and consistent, apply pressure, and NEVER let up. We may be the rookies but don't let them sleep on us. Ya'll know the goal, it's goin be a hot one. Turn up the heat all summer 16!

To my KBC sisters thank ya'll for keeping me motivated and always supporting me. And let me never forget all the tips ya'll provide for my sex scenes lol.

To my test readers, India, Jae, Kida, Kelly, Keondria, Krystal and Secret thanks for your brutal honesty and the late night group messages. You ladies provide laughter and keep me going when I am on empty. If I haven't sent something in a while I can depend on ya'll messaging me to see if all is well. Thank you forever.

The support didn't go unnoticed Ashley, Kristen, Feckey, Nakiala, Niqua, Yoshi and Puchi. Thank ya'll for the constant repost and the encouraging words. If I forgot someone charge it to my memory and not my heart.

To everyone who has shared a post, liked a post, promoted my release, congratulated me, etc this next one is for you. To my dear friend, (Say your name here) thank you a million times, you didn't have to rock with your girl but you did; and for that I will forever keep you entertained.

Kellz Rookieandthevet Kimberly Lol. You know your middle name changes at least three times a day. I couldn't ask for a better publisher than you if I wanted to. I can call at any time (unless you're on your granny flow and pass out at 9) to vent, cry or be petty and your right there in your Remy Ma voice going, "Paris, Paris, Trenae its fine. Take a break then come back to it. You are a dope writer don't force it." You are an amazing mentor and friend Kellz and I appreciate the hell out of you!! I tell you all the time but you took a chance on me and I'm rocking with you for the long haul. Let's make them put some respek on Kellz Kimberly Publishing. KKP is going to the top!

Last but most certainly not least, to my beautiful readers; I love each and every one of ya'll for rocking with me. You definitely didn't have to and that's what makes your support that more meaningful. I read every single review, comment, message, snapchat Dm and text message feedback you all gave and I used it. I value your opinions and appreciate you and them. Right here right now I give my word to remain consistent and keep you entertained. I'm back again with the characters you love so buckle up and prepare for this ride with Sin.

Connect with Trenae' on her various social media platforms:

Instagram: @Pardonmypetty

Facebook: Author Trenae

Facebook Reader's Group: Lipstick & Tea With Trenae'

Twitter: Oh_Paree_Dear

Periscope: Pardonmypetty

Snapchat: Pareetrenae

Chapter 1

Sinaya

"Though I'm missing you,

I'll find a way to get through,

Living without you…

Cause you were my sister, my strength and my pride…"

As I tuned out the sweet angelic voice, I couldn't stop the tears that were flowing behind the oversized Jackie O sunglasses that sat on my face. Nothing could have prepared me for burying a loved one, again. I guess this was karma coming back to bite me in the ass for all the bodies I had accumulated over time. Looking over at the two caskets nearly caused me to collapse. Something came over me and I needed to be near the caskets. I guess, in a strange way, it made me feel like Blessing and I were together again. I headed towards the Barbie sized pink casket first, where my sweet Neema lied resting eternally. Being that a bullet ripped through Blessing's stomach, Neema didn't have the chance to enter this cruel world. I sat in front of her closed casket and found myself breaking down. How could life be so selfish to take them both away from me, even if it was temporary? I heard an ear splitting scream and it hadn't registered that it was coming from me, until Ghost pulled me into his arms.

"No, I can't lose Blessing, I can't. If we have to bury her, then you will have to bury me too. I can't take anymore losses

1

Ghost, I can't. I wasn't even talking to her. She didn't know that I still loved her. I never told her." I cried in a voice I didn't remember. It had been a month since the shooting and these were my first words since then.

"I know baby; you talk to her every day and Blessing knew you loved her," he whispered in my ear, rocking me back and forth. I finally let my eyes land on the massive white casket and felt my knees buckle. After all that we've been through, I couldn't believe that I had to plan and attend her funeral. Annette and Blessing were the reasons I was able to get through my mom's funeral and all I wanted was to be able to lean on Blessing's shoulder to cry, and I couldn't; no one would be here to tell me that it would be ok this time. I finally brought my eyes to the white casket and my eyes landed on her beautiful face. Calmness came across me at that exact moment. I stood up and made my way over to her and began wiping imaginary lint from her Blazer. She looked like money in her two-piece, cocaine white Chanel pantsuit that matched mine, with the exception of the silver buttons; I had changed mine to gold. The red peep toe red bottoms she was wearing could not be seen because half of the casket was closed. Although you couldn't see hers, Neema was rocking the same custom made suit with a pair of red, soft bottom Louboutin flats. It cost a fortune to get that made, but her mom would have wanted nothing but the best for her, so I made it happen. We had all always said whoever went first, the others were supposed to make sure they were buried like a legend, so it was only right I brought the city out.

"Oh there were so many things,

That we could have shared,

If time was on our side.

Now that you're gone, I can still feel you near

So I'll smile with every tear I cry."

As the song ended, I watched as the pastor came over to say a few words about a woman he never met. Yes, we knew there was a God and definitely believed in him, but we weren't members of any church. Sometimes, I felt like the bigger sin would be for me to enter church, knowing I might catch a body on my way home. The way I saw it was I was wrong for playing God, but these were the cards I was dealt. My family needed to eat and I was the provider. I even faulted myself for getting Blessing and Rock caught up in this lifestyle, but what's done was done. Speaking of Rock, I missed him so much it hurt. For some reason or another, he pushed me away and here I was with no family left at the worst time. I figured he was grieving in his own way. Ghost nudging me pulled me from my thoughts, as I realized the services were over. Here was the part I dreaded, the final goodbye. How was I saying good-bye to my godchild and I had never even said hello? I guess that's a part of the hand I was dealt also; you win some and you lose some, but I refused to fold.

After kissing Neema's casket, I made my way to the bigger one of the two. Kissing her cold hard cheek for the last time, I dropped the red rose in her casket, adjusted my shades, and reached for Ghost and Streetz's hand as we left out the church. Streetz, like the rest of us, hadn't been himself since the shooting. The absence of Blessing and his daughter, Neema, had drastically changed him. Gone was the playful jokester and a fucking problem was left in his wake. I had been keeping a close eye on him because his ass was costing me money by killing all my damn workers and, if I didn't feel his pain, I would have killed him by now. As I made my way to the massive wooden doors of the church, my eyes landed on a group of men sitting in the back with shades on. They were sticking out like a sore thumb because they were in black and the dress code was all white. That's taking disrespect to a whole nother level. I felt Streetz's body go stiff as he attempted to pull away from me so, with a nod of my head, Murder and Gutta pulled him out the doors and into the awaiting town car. I knew he wouldn't be able to handle this and I didn't blame him; if I were in my right mind, I wouldn't be able to handle it either, but when have I ever been in my right mind?

After tapping the hood and watching the town car bend the corner, I kissed Ghost and we went to separate vehicles. I headed towards the black Tahoe that was awaiting and changed into a basic, black pants suit, pinned my hair up, and slipped on a black wig that was cut into a bob with bangs. After about 30 minutes of waiting, the back door was opened and my guest of honor entered with a man leading the way.

"To the new headquarters please?" the man asked as they got settled in the back. I drove for about an hour with another Tahoe following closely behind me, until we reached a warehouse. There was whispering going on in the back, but I wasn't concerned with that; my mind was back on Blessing. This past month without my sister and niece had been almost unbearable. Ghost, Noelle, and Breeze helped me hold it together but, being honest, they just weren't Blessing. Pulling up to the location, I waited for my vehicle's occupants to step out just as the second Tahoe pulled in, and they all entered the building. After a brief moment, I exited the vehicle just as Ghost stepped out of his and we joined hands as we walked into the warehouse. The clicking of my heels announced our presence before I could and all heads turned towards us.

"Gentleman, thanks for meeting me here." I strolled in and walked right up to Emmanuel's face with Ghost by my side. "I heard you have been looking all over for Sin; well, here I am live and in living color," I said as he smirked.

"Even prettier than your sister was before I killed her and that bastard child; at least she gets to join your mother again. It is a shame-" was all he got out before he was knocked on his ass. I looked at Ghost and shook my head. Lately, he had gotten a hell of a lot worse than me with his temper. Looking around at who Emmanuel thought were loyal men, I had to laugh; they knew him for years and a lil money made them all jump ship. Come to find out, he treated them more as servants than family; they'd wanted to jump ship for a while but feared the repercussions, so I got rid of their problem and the money I offered was just an added bonus.

"Tie him to that chair." I nodded towards the torture chair I had delivered for this very reason a few weeks ago. After he was tied

5

up, I slipped on a protective suit and some goggles, then grabbed the chainsaw that was waiting. Nodding at Ghost, I watched as Emmanuel jumped up gasping for air, after he poured a bucket of water over his head. If I wasn't so pissed off, this might have been funny to me. After calming himself, I watched as his eyes looked at his men in what appeared to be shock, then anger as they connected with mine. I couldn't help the smirk that graced my face.

"Nice nap you took there, grandfather."

"You are of no relation to me, orphan bitch! Do you know who the fuck I am? Bitch, I will burn your ass alive for this shit!" he spat, making me laugh loudly.

"Now, that is a genius idea grandfather! I was gonna chop you up and ship that ass back to Haiti, but your shit sounds nice." I looked over at Ghost. "Bae, we have some gas in this bitch?" I asked.

"Yeah, we do." I looked up at the voice and shook my head at Rello, as he licked his lips and stared me down. He was a new nigga that we brought on the squad and he had a lil crush on me. He and Ghost stayed coming to blows and I tried to save him because his ass was bringing me in more money than my money machines could count. Looking him over, I forced myself not to lick my lips. Rello knew his young ass was some kind of fine and, if I didn't have a man, I might let his ass ride this ride. I always had a thing for chocolate and he was a double serving of that shit. Standing at about 6'5" and about 225 pounds with more tats than Lil Wayne, this man was definitely someone I was staying far away from. I couldn't help but to silently give my approval over his fit; I knew this wasn't your average lil nigga. He was rocking a pair of black, distressed True Religion jeans that sagged a little under his waist, despite the matching True Religion belt, a black True Religion hoodie, and a pair of black and gold high top Giuseppe tennis shoes. And staring at his waves had a bitch sea sick; shout out to his barber cause his lining was so crisp. I'm convinced God cut that shit.

"Nigga, since when my bitch call you bae? Keep fucking licking those ashy ass lips at her and watch them bitches get shot the fuck off. Make that the last time you fucking answer when she's talking to me; I done told you that shit before!" Ghost snapped but the smirk never left Rello's face.

"Aye, that's all you, boss man. My fault." He chuckled and raised his hands in mock surrender, pulling a blunt from behind his ear. I didn't realize I was still watching his every move until our eyes connected and he licked his plump lips at me, immediately causing me to fuck up my panties. Looking away, I felt the color rush to my cheeks. I would never intentionally disrespect Ghost, but god damn if I wasn't cheating in my head. Ghost must have caught the look that Rello gave me because Ghost's ass was making his way over to him, like I wasn't trying to kill my dear old grandpa here. Mello followed my eyes to Ghost, put the blunt back behind his ears, and pulled his pants up on his waist. If you know anything about the hood, then you know that meant shit was going down.

Shaking my head, I looked back at Emmanuel, who had a pocket knife and was trying to break the lock on the chair. I slowly made my way over and squatted in front of him without his knowledge.

"Fuck is you doing pawpaw?" I taunted. When he spit in my direction, I simply nodded and walked to the back to grab a canister of gas.

"I should have been killed you, but at least I got one and a half of you bitches." He laughed, giving up on the lock. "You know this shit won't end because you've killed me, right? You're starting a war that you can't win alone." He laughed as I finished throwing the gas over his body. Lighting a blunt, I walked over to get a fire extinguisher and returned in front of him as I smoked my blunt. Turning around, I saw all eyes were back on me; I guess the men stopped the fight. I could have stopped them, but it was a respect thing. I would never test my man's gangster in front of our workers, even if I was the boss. Hitting the blunt once more, I turned to face Emmanuel once again.

"You seem like a smart man, so let me ask you something. Why would I have Neema's funeral with Annette if Blessing was really dead?" I smirked when his eyes opened in shock. "You see, grandfather, you couldn't compete with me because you can't compare to me. I'm a fucking boss in the states. You should have kept your wrinkled ass in Haiti if you wanted to run some shit." I blew a kiss as I threw the blunt on top of him. I could have passed him through the incinerator and been done with him, but that didn't seem as fun. I listened as his screams filled the building, then nodded at the men to put him out before I pulled out Blessing's twin Berettas and emptied the clip in his ass.

Chapter 2

Blessing

Opening my eyes seemed like a task within itself. I had been trying for what felt like days and, now that I've finally opened them, I wish I hadn't. I didn't remember everything, but I knew I was shot a few times, but the pain that surged through my body had nothing to do with those pussy ass gun shots. Last I remembered, I was pregnant and here I was with a perfectly flat stomach. The more I thought about my daughter, or the lack of, the more I started to lose it. I tried to remember everything that led to me being here, but my mind went blank after Annette caught me sneaking up the staircase. I remember learning of her lies, but I knew I was forgetting something really important, I just couldn't remember what and that was pissing me off. Why the fuck hadn't a nurse walked in yet? My frustrations were amplified when I realized I couldn't swing my legs off of the bed because they were attached to a machine that was vibrating, so I settled for pressing the nurse's call button. Instead of answering the button, a beautiful nurse strolled in the room with a warm smile.

"I'm glad you're back with us, Blessing. I've been your nurse for the duration of your stay. I'm sure you have questions for me but, first, the doctor will come in to remove that tube from down your throat," she spoke as the door was opened by an older attractive doctor.

"Blessing, I'm happy you decided to grace us with your presence. I am Dr. Pollard, a colleague of your father. I am going to remove this aggravating tube; now, this will be a little uncomfortable but, then, we can give you some ice and water." I nodded as he removed the tube from my throat and handed me a cup of water. The cold water was welcoming to my burning throat. After finishing the cup, I cleared my throat and asked the questions I'd been dying to know.

"How long have I been here?" I managed to whisper.

"A little over a month; you've been really popular with the visitors." The nurse smiled as she checked my blood pressure.

"And what ab- about my baby." I knew what she would tell me, but I had to know for sure for myself.

"Oh, your baby is healthy and, well, the little sweetheart left with your sister after two weeks of being hospitalized." When she answered that, tears immediately fell from my eyes; I wasn't too happy about having a baby at first, but I couldn't wait to lay my eyes on her. Did she look like Streetz or was she a mini me?

"Yeah, they're usually here around the clock, but she said they would be here later in the day. She always brings the baby to lie on your chest when it's sleepy. And your godchild is forever talking your head off." She chuckled

"That's my diva." I laughed.

"Your boyfriend should be in here shortly; I just saw him down the hall, leaving the cafeteria."

"My boyfriend? I know I've been out for a while, but I don't remember having a boyfriend." I looked at her, confused.

11

"Tall, bright with dreads, and very mean." She giggled

"Oh Streetz, do me a favor and don't tell him I'm up. In fact, don't tell anyone I'm up just yet. Can I have more water?" I asked, holding out my cup.

Of course you can." As she walked out to get more water, the door swung open and Streetz walked in. Before he could look my way, I quickly closed my eyes. I wasn't sure how to approach a conversation with him, so I wasn't. Last time we spoke, he wasn't anything but my baby's father and, if our daughter went home, then why was he here? Speaking of my daughter, I hoped it was my sister who named her and not Streetz because I would fucking lose it if my daughter was named after him. Knowing his ass, he would want her to be nicknamed Jr. and all. I felt him standing over me and the scent from his cologne still started the flow of the river between my legs. When he bent down to kiss my lips, I tried to control my breathing, but the damn machines gave me away and started beeping. He quickly pulled back, then called for the nurse who walked in and asked him to step out.

"Are you ok Blessing?" she asked.

"Yeah, you brought that water in?" I whispered back, knowing Streetz was right outside the door. Reaching behind her, she grabbed the cup of water and handed it to me, as she looked over the machines once again.

"Are we still playing charades?" she asked.

"Yep, let the doctors know also. I don't want anyone but Sinaya knowing I'm up."

"Ok, let me step out and get him for you." I listened to her leave and felt when he stepped in the room seconds later.

"You need to get your ass up and stop faking Blessing," I wanted to whip the nurse's ass because I knew she had outed me until he kept going, "shit is all wrong without you, ma. They say that when ya'll in a coma, ya'll can hear us and shit, so I'm wondering why you haven't answered a nigga's pleas yet. I know your ass be laughing cause you got my grown ass crying over you and shit, but it's good shorty; this your world right now. On the real Blessing, this shit been fucking with me bad. This shit right here is all on me; I was mad at your ass for keeping my baby a secret, when I should have been cherishing you. Now, your stubborn ass won't give me the chance to make this shit up. We have a baby to raise and your ass wanna sleep all day." He took a long pause and I felt him stand up and walk on the other side of me, and I heard the sound of him flipping through papers. Then, after a few moments, he sat back down. "Aye but, on the real B, I'm kind of glad you're in this coma bullshit or whatever because I haven't found the words to let you know the shit that's been going on. Besides ours, a nigga has another youngin that's turning one in a few months. I've known about him but, shit, I'm thinking of marrying his mom and wanted our child to live with her and me." I felt his hair tickle my arm as he placed his head on the bed, and I found strength I didn't know was there when I grabbed a handful of his dreads.

"Nigga, you must have me confused with that other bitch, playing with me like I'm pussy." I tightened my grip on his dreads. "A fucking baby though, Juelz? And you think you just goin take my child and play house with the bitch, nigga? I'll have that bitch eating a full clip since you wanna try me and shit. Don't let this hospital bed make you forget how I give it up!" I spat. It took a moment for me to stop seeing red and realize that he was laughing. "You better be thinking of some shit Kevin Hart said cause I don't see a damn thing funny." I know I was out for a while, but Streetz didn't look the same to me. The bags under his eyes and unkempt dreads didn't take away from how fucking fine he was though. I noticed he was wearing the hell out of an all-white suit and I would inquire about that later because that nigga dressed as street as his name led on.

"Yo, I thought some rest would calm your ass down; how the fuck you wake up from that long ass nap spazzing on the kid?" he asked, standing up and still laughing like I wasn't on ten over here.

"Aye, do me a favor real quick?" I asked him calmly.

"Wassup, you hurting? You need me to call the nurse?" A look of concern covered his face.

"Nah, bring you mixed breed ass closer, so I can rock your dumb ass. Nigga, you got me all kinds of fucked up if you think you're marrying some bitch. Should have done that shit while I was out of commission pimp, cause let me hear a word of this and I'm lighting up the fucking church."

14

"You know where your ass going after you do that shit?" he asked, cracking up.

"Oh, I know I'll go straight to hell behind that and I'll take that charge cause even the pastor catching a bullet for trying me. Juelz, you have another fucking baby son?" I asked, trying to stop the tears from falling. My heart was really breaking; I didn't want to front anymore. I needed Streetz like I needed air.

"Shit, you can't trip; you didn't want a nigga huh, she did?" he asked.

"Juelz, call Sin and ask her why I got kicked out of preschool. Nah, I'll tell you, for beating a thotler's ass for thinking we could share my shit. I've never grown out of the mind frame of what's mine is mine, so I'll tell you once; dead that shit before I have to. And when I say I'll dead something, I'm talking black dresses, slow walking, and loud crying daddy," I said, staring him in the eyes.

"So, I'm yours Blessing?" he smirked.

"You ain't know love? Now, about this baby, real bitches do real things, so we'll have her sign over her rights to us and raise two babies." Him crying laughing stopped me from continuing with my lil speech. "Something funny Juelz?"

"Yo, how the fuck you just plan to steal someone's child? You are real life fucking crazy," he said, grabbing his stomach and laughing until he realized he was laughing alone. I was dead ass

15

serious about raising his other kid. "Chill son, ain't no other kid or bitch; I knew your funky ass was up."

"You a lie and a half, how did you know?"

"First, that big ass tube they were feeding you that stank shit through is gone, there is a fresh cup of water sitting on your nightstand, and I kiss your ass everyday but, today, a nigga had you all hot and bothered, setting off machines and shit," he smirked as I flicked him off. I really looked him over and realized that, despite the suit he was rocking, Streetz looked bad, real bad.

"Have you gone to see our daughter today? She looks like your ugly ass, doesn't she?" I fake pouted. I expected him to laugh or even crack a joke back, but what I didn't expect were the tears that escaped from his eyes. "Damn, you aren't that ugly, what's wrong?" I joked, even though I was worried.

"Blessing, there is no real way to tell you this; we tried to hold off as long as we could, but she couldn't just sit there in her condition." He looked everywhere but at me.

"Streetz, spit that shit out; what's wrong with my baby?" I grew impatient.

"One of the bullets went through your stomach, Blessing; today, we buried Annette and Neema," were the last words I heard before the machines started beeping and everything went black.

Chapter 3

Young

"Aimee, you look fine ma; chill with all that greasy shit and get out the car. A nigga been on that damn plane all morning and my stomach on e." We had just touched down in Cali, and it was hotter than a bitch and a nigga was starving. Between my girl Aimee, and my sister, Sunjai, they were both about to piss me off, getting done up just so we could go in funky ass Red Lobster.

"Young, don't rush perfection. I might run into a boss in here," Aimee said, enough for me to choke her ass out. I quickly walked over to her side of the car and snatched it open before she could hit the locks.

"Nah, don't lock the door, talk that shit nah. I didn't hear you from over there; don't make me show my ass Me-Me. That's why that blue lipstick look a fucking mess. Looks like you been sucking poppa smurf dick," I said, dodging the weak ass punch she threw my way, as she climbed out the car and fixed her shorts. I looked Aimee over and couldn't help but to smile at her thick ass. Standing at 5'4" and 155 pounds, she resembled a taller, more stacked Lira Galore, with the exception of her hair; she was bald like Wiz's baby mama, Amber Rose.

"Nah son, don't look this way with that crooked ass smile cause you ain't digging in my honey pot for a few days. Get well acquainted with your hand Junior," she added emphasis on the Junior part cause she knew I hated being called that shit.

17

"Bet that up, we both know after I rub your lumpy ass at night, you going be begging me to go balls deep in them guts," I threw back, pinning her to the car door when I heard banging on the car hood.

"Ya'll so damn disrespectful, just fuck out here why don't cha," Sunjai's annoying ass said, climbing out of the backseat of my car.

"Sis, you just need some zickkkk," Aimee said, sticking out her pierced tongue. I wanted to smack the shit out her freaky ass, talking to my sister like that.

"What, fuck no she don't! Play with it if you want to Sunjai, but I'm bodying everything that looks your way. Your ass better stay like they found you, pure!" I was so overprotective of her that you would think I was the big brother. Sunjai and I were fraternal twins, but she was the older by five punk ass minutes and never let me forget it.

"Shut yo ass up Sincere. I don't know why you think that girl is still a virgin; with that ass and those hips baby, she throwing that ass like a quarterback." Aimee slapped hands with my sister before running away before I could choke her ass out. They knew I didn't find shit about what she just said funny; like I said, I was bodying any nigga that looked at my sister.

Better ask about her high school prom date, Rodney. Nigga thought he had a friend when he confided in my cousin that he had already rented a room for the night cap. I left Aimee's ass in the shower of our hotel room and paid the attendant to let me in the one Rodney had booked. Nigga had that shit laid out with candles, chocolates, massage oils, champagne, chocolate covered strawberries, and roses. Shit was real player like and Rodney was going all out for some ass he wasn't getting. I heard him coming in the room and hid in the bathroom. God was on my side because Sunjai decided to drive, so he beat her to the room, then had the nerve to be bragging about his plans on the phone to someone. I burst out that bathroom in a mighty duck costume; I'm talking the jersey, mask, and a fucking hockey stick. I beat his ass all around the room with that damn stick too. Nigga could barely get up, yet along touch my sister. Before I left, I grabbed a pillowcase and took all his shit. I walked in my room and placed the candles, chocolates, massage oils, champagne, chocolate covered strawberries, and roses just like he had it set up. Aimee's ass just knew I was being romantic and she threw that fat ass back all fucking night; I never did get to thank Rodney. They sent his ass away when he kept telling the cops a mighty duck whipped his ass. Aimee found out about it when she found the mask in my car, so her ass knew how I felt about any nigga around Sunjai.

"Yeah alright, Sunjai, you keep thinking that shit funny and watch how I tell pops yo ass be acting with Aimee freak ass!" I said, knowing if I choked her, she would pull out one of those damn knives and cut me, again. My fucking arm was just healing from the last cut.

"How you call your own woman a freak, Young?"

19

"Shit, why you think she my woman? Aimee can't ever leave cause my ass spoiled. How you think her ass got that new Benz," I said with no smile. I was dead ass serious too. Sunjai had a fascination for cars, so she was forever getting her a new car and Aimee's ass just had to be right on side of her. When Sunjai got her matte black Benz, here come Aimee bowlegged ass walking over, talking about she needed one. I told her ass no until she had my dick getting tickled by her tonsils and that long ass lizard tongue was licking my balls. Next thing I knew, her ass had my black card and a cocaine white Benz. Looking down, I saw my dick getting hard just from the thought of that day, and I had to think of some other shit before my dick beat me in this building.

As soon as we walked into the restaurant, my eyes landed on this shorty that was killing the fuck out of a pantsuit and I couldn't look away if I wanted to. She owned the room and walked; nah, what she had wasn't a walk. Lil mama had a strut, like she owned the room. I guess she felt my eyes on her behind her shades, so she looked in my direction until she quickly looked behind her at some tall nigga with dreads. The smile on her face wasn't missed when she looked at him and all I could think was damn, he was a lucky nigga, as they held hands.

WHAP!

"Aimee, what the fuck I said about putting your fucking hands on me?" I asked, rubbing the back of my head. A nigga had just got a fresh cut before we flew in, so that shit really stung from her slap.

20

"Keep watching the bitch and that lil slap will be the least of your problems!" she snapped. The couple had to pass us up to head towards the parking lot and I was hoping Aimee didn't say shit cause she was known to get shit started with females and niggas. I wasn't scared of not one nigga walking, well, except my pops, so I would throw down if this nigga disrespected my bitch, but the size of him led me to believe it would be a workout. I didn't know if I was more shocked that she didn't say anything or the fact that the chick did.

"Do yourself a favor and watch that bitch word, lil mama; your man peeped me, not the other way around. That was your first and only warning, besides, my pussy only gets wet for one nigga, so you have nothing to fear but catching these hands if you call me out my name again." She winked, leaving Aimee speechless for the first time ever.

***

After Aimee caught her bitch fit on me and refused to talk while we ate, we all headed to the hospital to meet up with my pops. He had gotten the call that my newly found sister, Blessing, woke up from her coma, so he asked us to skip the unpacking for now and get this meeting out of the way.

"What's good old man," I said, hugging him.

"Watch that old word; I'll still whip your ass Young," he said, playfully jabbing me in the stomach.

"Daddy!" Sunjai screamed, running up and hugging him as he spun her around. Sunjai knew her ass was too old for that shit; she was the definition of a daddy's girl. They normally have breakfast together every morning so, when he left to get settled out here, her spoiled ass was lonely.

"Your fat ass goin' fuck around and break pops back with that jumping on him shit." I nodded my head as Aimee childish ass walked over, pouting.

"What's wrong Me-Me?" Aimee was like a daughter to pops, so she knew exactly what she was doing when she walked her bald ass over here.

"Ain't shit, she pissed off cause there was this bad ass female in Red Lobster that embarrassed her slick head ass. Pops, you should have seen that shit, had Aimee ghetto ass on hush."

"Shut the fuck up Young! That shit wasn't even funny; you shouldn't have disrespected Me-Me like that nigga," Sunjai said, grilling me.

"Disrespect her how, by looking at a bitch? Fuck, Stevie Wonder and Ray Charles could tell lil mama was bad, but Aimee gotta stop with that insecure shit son. She can't put my eyes in her fucking purse every time a bad bitch walks by; I'm a nigga. I'm goin look."

"Alright, bet that up Young; we both goin fuck around and try something new," Aimee smirked.

"Come see Aimee," I said, walking towards her, "I ain't heard that shit; come closer, so I can answer you back." I was ready to choke life from her ass.

22

"Young, chill, you're in front of a hospital," my pops said as he protected Aimee, who ran behind his back.

"Perfect place for them to bring her ass back from the light, so I can choke her out again; you keep playing super save a hoe pops and watch-"

"Watch what Sincere?" his booming voice interrupted me. I smacked my teeth and mugged his old ass. He lucky I know his aim game official or I would steal off on him.

"Watch when your ancient ass gets too old, your ass goin' end up in a low budget nursing home. Like it's going to be so low budget, it won't have a name, just nursing home. I'll pay them not to turn your old ass over and you goin have bed sores," I said as he was cracking up.

"My daddy ain't going in no nursing home nigga." Sunjai said, mugging my head.

"So, you called us here to stand outside? What, don't tell me you nervous all of a sudden old school?" I asked my pops, laughing.

"For ya'll to meet Blessing, hell no. She's actually excited to meet ya'll. And I'm glad she's finally up. But ya'll oldest sister is another story. They said her ass is worse than me, so I know she's goin flip out when she sees us in that room. Let's get up there; I know ya'll want to get settled in," he said, leading us up to the room. Walking in, my eyes immediately fell on the nigga that was occupying the bed my sister should have been in.

"Streetz, what's good; where is my daughter?" Pops asked him.

"Oh, what's up, she's in the bathroom getting herself together," Streetz answered while still lying in the bed.

"By herself?" Sunjai asked, already heading towards the door like she knew Blessing. That's just how my sister was, always worried about the next person.

"Nah, the nurse in there; I was trying to help but she kicked me out," Streetz answered as the bathroom door swung open and the nurse walked out, followed by who I assumed was Blessing. She didn't notice we were in the room because we were positioned behind the door.

"You good baby mama, you look a hell of a lot better," Streetz said, making me look at my father. He ain't told me she had a child, yet along that it was with Streetz. I wouldn't necessarily call him a legend in the game but, when speaking of bosses, his name was mentioned often. So, although I didn't know him, I definitely knew of him.

"Yeah with no help from your mannish ass." She laughed.

"Hey, I tried helping; you kicked me out. You been so damn mean since you woke up. Maybe you need a nap, just wake your ass up this time," Streetz answered back, laughing at his own joke. I looked at his low, bloodshot red eyes and knew he was high.

"Nigga, cause your ass was talking about seeing if my pussy still got wet after being in a coma for a month. The Nile still flows

24

just fine daddy," she said, causing me to frown up my face but Aimee and Sunjai to laugh.

"Nah, you have one daddy in this fucking room," my pops said with humor in his voice. "Streetz, you better leave my daughter the fuck alone nigga; she just waking up," he said as Blessing pushed the door completely opened and noticed us for the first time.

"Oh my God, Streetz, you ain't shit for not warning me. Daddy, I was just joking," she said, laughing as Streetz stood up to carry her to the bed.

"Yeah, I bet you were; hey, I know we Facetimed before, but it's so crazy to actually meet my sister." Sunjai went over and hugged her, so I followed.

"And, of course, my handsome ass is Young," I clowned, hugging her and shaking Streetz's hand.

"Hey girl, I'm Aimee, but you can call me Me-Me like everyone else; I'm Young's girlfriend," Aimee introduced herself and hugged her also.

"Hey, I'm Blessing, nice meeting you in person." She returned the hugs. After all introductions were made, I initially assumed it would be awkward, but the conversation really flowed as we got to know each other.

We kicked back and vibed for a while until the room door swung open once again. I didn't bother looking up because nurses had been in and out for the past hour.

"What the fuck is this bitch doing here?" Aimee asked, causing me to look up from my phone into the black eyes of the female from Red Lobster.

"Aww shit, this will be good," Streetz said, lying against the pillows in the bed. "Sorry Young, but I got a stack on Sin; she doesn't take to kind to that bitch word and sis got a killer right hook."

Chapter 4

Sinaya

"So, you're really just gone walk past your people like you don't know them?" Ghost asked as we left Red lobster.

"Well, I don't know them, now do I?" I said with an attitude. For days, Ghost's ass had been pressuring to talk to my father and the only thing I was willing to make talk was my guns. I fucked around and did some research, and now I had four bullets for four different people, but I was just going to sit on that information right now. My bigger issue was Rock; I hardly saw him these days. I thought he was grieving in his own way, but his ass didn't even make the funeral this morning.

"I already told you watch your fucking tone when speaking to a boss, Sinaya. How are you feeling about everything?"

"Everything like what Deion?" I knew he was speaking on the whole Annette situation and I didn't want to talk about it yet. After the shooting, I went to the house and retrieved the tapes. I knew exactly what went on, but I wasn't speaking on that either, at least not now.

"Sin, you don't think it's time to tell me what were on those tapes?" he asked, biting his lip. That was something I'd learned he did when he's upset with me. If I was anyone else, his rude ass would have called me all kinds of bitches and hoes right now.

"Let me figure everything out and I will tell you every single detail," I said, pulling out my kindle to read *When Loving You Is a Crime* by this new author Bianca Marie; baby girl was wicked with a pen. I'd picked up reading recently to escape this bullshit I called life. I'm blessed with material things and more money than man needs, but my family was as dysfunctional as they come. Within this last month, I had completely zoned out on all of our businesses if it didn't include catching a body. For a brief moment, killing people was taking my mind off the bullshit that I was caught up in. Ghost and Streetz had been holding down our illegal operations and I had some trusted employers overseeing the legal operations. I was dealing with possibly losing my sister, raising a newborn, raising Breeze, trying to get Noelle to her old self, the death of the only mother I remembered, and the niece I would never meet. Oh and with me passing out, Noelle's sperm donor was able to escape once again. On top of that, I felt like I was losing Ghost. Call it a woman's intuition if you will, but shit wasn't sitting right. A woman knows when a man changes up; we study our men. Ghost wasn't moving like himself, but I was treating him like court, innocent until proven guilty.

***

"Hey Ms. Lee Ann and Breeze, has Noelle eaten anything today?" I asked the live-in nanny that I hired to help while I got myself together.

"Hello Sinaya, you look beautiful and, yes, she has eaten already. She is really coming around; I have to watch her. She likes sneaking into Noah's room and trying to climb in bed with him," she answered, shaking her head and laughing. I could already tell Noelle and Noah would have a bond like Blessing and I did. He was helping her come out of her funk, just like Blessing had helped me. Sometimes when he would cry in the middle of the night, she would beat me to the room and already had a bottle sitting in the bottle warmer. She was confused for a moment because she knew Blessing was having a daughter and, instead, we brought home a son and I had to explain to her that Neema went to heaven, while Noah was able to stay here with us. Turns out, Noah was hiding behind Neema and we didn't know Blessing was expecting twins until the emergency C-section. Now, I have to fight Noelle and Breeze so that I can hold him.

"I know she thinks that he's her responsibility until Blessing wakes up. Just make sure she doesn't climb in the bed with him. Other than that, she can stay there if it'll make her come around," I said, flipping through the mail.

"Rough night last night?" she asked, looking over the rim of her glasses. Ms. Lee Ann was approaching 50 years old but didn't look a day over 40. "I heard you crying out again at around 3. I came to check on you but Ghost was walking in, so I went back to sleep. I'm praying for you though, your sister too," she said, causing me to nod my head.

"I appreciate it. It's just everything going on with Blessing is hard; my sister is waking up soon though. I can feel that much," I said with more assurance in my tone than I felt in my heart. Walking up the stairs, I watched as Ghost quickly hung up his phone, as I made my way to our adjourning bathroom and stripped down for a bath. Hooking my phone to the Bluetooth speaker, I went to my old school playlist and placed my phone on the sink. After running the bath water and throwing in a lush bomb, I quickly showered, then walked over to the bathtub and melted in the warmth. Call me crazy if you want to, but I refuse to sit in today's dirt. Closing my eyes, I sang along to TLC as they explained why they creeped, until I felt eyes on me.

"Did you leave to go to your house last night?" I asked without opening my eyes. Although Ghost was here every day and night, he still kept his home and I had this one and the condo.

"No, I slept here," he quickly answered.

"All night?"

"Is there a reason you're asking this?" he dodged my question, causing me to open my eyes and make eye contact with him that I noticed he kept breaking.

"No reason. I just remember rolling over and the bed was empty at around three; I may have been dreaming though." I finished and began singing aloud with the song. "I love my man with all honesty, but I know he's cheating on me. I look him in his eyes, but all he tells me is lies to keep me near."

"Yo Red, we good right?" he asked, finally looking at me as I my phone rang. I no longer had the urge to stay in the house, so I got out the tub and answered the phone, praying for an excuse to leave.

Nothing could prepare me for the news I did hear; Blessing was up and talking. Ignoring Ghost, I quickly dried off and got dressed. I felt Ghost's eyes watching me as I lotioned myself with my Bath and Body Works, Mad About You, then slipped on a red lace bra and thong set. I quickly threw my hair in a high bun and grabbed some gold hoops and my gold Rolex. Throwing on a wine colored maxi dress and some gold gladiator sandals, I knew he would flip because he hates when I wear maxi dresses and thongs because of how much my ass jiggles.

"Red, where are we going and I asked you a question."

"Oh yeah, you did huh?" I asked, laughing at his clown ass. "Oh and the kids and I are stepping out; you aren't coming though because you should be tired, right? You were, after all, out and about at 3 in the morning."

"How the fuck you tell me where I can and can't go? I'm grown as the fuck!" he roared. I knew him like the back of my hand at this point and Ghost was mad because he knew his ass was cold busted. Like the song said, I love my man but I know he's cheating on me. Without any proof, I was just gonna act accordingly though.

"You're right; you can go wherever the fuck you decide to go, but I wish a motherfucker other than my kids hopped in my car. Watch what I do intruders."

"Where the fuck this all coming from Sin? We was cool a second ago."

"Nothing's wrong but, I promise you this, let me find some proof of anything and I will be playing monkey see monkey do." I hit his ass with the deuce, and my babies and I headed to the hospital. Stopping by the nurse's desk, I spoke to the nurses and was informed Blessing had visitors, and I was ready to bet my last dollar on who that was. Speaking with the doctor, we decided to leave Noah in the nursery until I broke the news to Blessing about Neema. Streetz promised that he would let me do it, but I honestly think he's actually just scared to be the one to tell her. Making my way to the room with Breeze and Noelle following me, I walked in the door as all eyes fell on me.

"What the fuck is this bitch doing here?" I cocked my head to the side because this was the second time this bitch called me out of my name today. My daughters were her saving grace.

I am more than my anger

I am more than my anger

I am more than my anger

"Is she crazy? I mean, she's over there talking to herself and shit." I heard the cute girl with dreads ask.

"Nah, lil mama, you might want to give her that and let her do her shit before we all be sporting bullet holes," Streetz answered, laughing.

"She's not the only one with a gun," the chick who called me a bitch decided to speak up.

"Nah, but I bet no one in this fucking room can make them thangs sang like I can. I'm goin let you know now that I'm not a liar. I warned you this morning that you were only getting one warning and you got that. This right here is me letting you know that you have an ass whipping on reserve. Anytime I see you and my kids aren't in my presence, it's on sight," I said. Noticing my daughters were hiding behind my legs, I lowered my tone.

"I respect that you're my lil brother's woman Aimee, but I guarantee you don't want it with her because you will have to want it with me too. What the fuck is the problem anyway?" Blessing asked, finally speaking and reminding me of why I rushed here.

"This dizzy broad just in her feelings because her nigga was looking at me earlier at Red Lobster, like I was stunting him or her," I said, mugging this Aimee chick and ignoring the rest of the visitors.

"Aunnniiieeee, you woke up. You was sleep longer than sleeping beauty. I told uncle Juelz to kiss you so you could wake up, but him said you mouth funky," Noelle said, running towards Blessing after peeping from around my legs and realizing that she was actually sitting up. I noticed the older man in the room stood to help her climb in the bed and I put a stop to that.

"Streetz, help my baby girl cause if another nigga puts his hand on my fucking daughter, I guarantee I will nut the fuck up in this bitch," I said, never taking my eyes off the man who raised his hand in surrender with a smirk placed on his face.

"Uh uh uncle Ju, you didn't even hug me and you hugging her," Breeze said, walking towards Streetz with her hands on her hips. She and Noelle were so damn womanish.

"Awww shit, this must be Sin," the chick with the dreads spoke again. "Hey I'm Sunjai, your lil sister." She held out her hand that I looked at, then finally shook it.

"Umm Sunjai, my sister is laid up in that bed and, besides her and Rock, I have no known siblings. Now, if you all would step out, I would like to speak with her." I didn't have a problem with her personally, but I'm far from friendly; yep, it was no new friends around here.

"Who the fuck you think you talking too?" the dude finally spoke.

"Nigga, I said you all! Fuck, I'm speaking to all ya'll. Blessing, you better let your brother, his jump off, your sister, and ya'll bitch ass father know how the fuck I give it up." I was pissed and it wasn't even at them. Ghost already had me on ten. I watched as Blessing calmed them down and asked them to leave the room. After they left, Streetz kissed Blessing and the girls before heading to the hallway and pulling me out of the door with him.

"Aye, you hell in a skirt." He laughed. "Umm, she asked about Neema and I told her, sort of. She passed out and doesn't remember the conversation, so you're on your own with that conversation, so you can hit her with that info again. I'm about to dip for a second; where you left Ghost?"

"Oh, he probably smiling in some bitch face; you know, the usual," I said, laughing. "Let me get to my sister, be safe," I said, walking back in the room.

"Well, I thought you would be happy to see me," Blessing said, smiling as the tears began falling from my eyes. I was frustrated and relieved all in one, but I would never show weakness in front of outsiders. I made my way onto the bed with Blessing and the girls, and we cried and hugged for what felt like hours. After getting ourselves together, she asked the question I wasn't prepared to answer.

"I missed you and all sis, but where is my daughter; what's her name?"

Chapter 5

Ghost

A nigga was stressing, walking into the warehouse. I was living foul as fuck, but I wasn't taking that charge by myself. Red had been slipping on her duties at home and a nigga was backed into a corner. Sinaya was my calm in these streets and, lately, I ain't been getting that from her. If I came home and wanted to discuss my day, she would blank out on me and then tell me she had enough on her mind already. She wasn't even spending time with our daughters; she hired a messy ass nanny. I know it wasn't anybody but her old ass told Sinaya what time I came home. The nanny was cooking, cleaning, and taking care of the girls. Then, to top it all off, Sin was holding out on the pussy. Sinaya had me spoiled; I had gotten accustomed to getting it however and whenever I wanted it, and she just stopped. I kid you not; I hadn't even smelled the pussy in three weeks, six days, four hours, and 36 seconds.

"Fuck is wrong with you, looking like you lost your best friend. Shit, I'm right here so what's really good?" Streetz asked, walking in and looking better than he had since the shooting. For someone who wasn't fucking with Blessing like that, I think he took her getting shot harder than Sinaya did.

"Ain't shit I can't handle. You look better, glowing and shit," I cracked, changing the subject.

"Oh yeah, Blessing woke up. I just left from up there; nigga, your gah wilding. She was snapping on niggas left and right for nothing. She called Sincere old ass a bitch nigga. You must not be giving her dick properly; she in there being meaner than a starving pit-bull."

"I can't give her dick when she's never home to receive it," I mumbled but Streetz, of course, heard that shit.

"Nigga, she is at the hospital 24 fucking 7. Where you expect her to be if her sister has been shot?" He looked at me like I had just made the dumbest statement. When it came to females and their emotions, Streetz was the nigga that knew everything. I didn't know anything about their emotions and all that soft shit, and that's why I fucked with Sin. She wasn't all soft. Before all this, she was one of the niggas, busting guns and breaking down work. Now, her eyes stayed puffy and red from crying, and she hasn't shown her face in the warehouse since that shooting, besides the funeral day.

"Nigga, you heard what the fuck I just said?" Streetz asked, snapping in my face.

"Nah, what's up?"

"I asked what's really good; when I asked her where you were, she told me probably smiling in some bitch face and started laughing. Nigga, like she laughed a crazy fucking laugh, not right in the head laugh. When I'm at the hospital, the t.v. always on lifestyle or Lifetime or some shit like that, and she looked like one of those bitches. Better watch it; she goin end up on snapped. But real shit, you cheating on sis?"

"Man, she thinks that I'm cheating on her, but-"

"Say less, nigga, I know when you're lying. All I'm goin say on that subject is if you're out here cheating because she taking care of her sister, you foul as fuck son. All they have is each other and, on some real shit, if the shoe was on the other foot, she would be there for you. Sinaya is the last of a dying breed of females; I hope you don't let some other nigga luck up on that one."

"Yeah, alright Dr. Phil; have you niggas found Snake and Ahmad bitch asses yet?" I asked, changing the subject.

"Tech and the crew about to come through with that info in a minute; check it though, how the fuck these niggas both just disappear like that? We can find niggas in the blink of an eye and here it is taking too fucking long for us to find their asses, and it ain't sitting right with me to be honest."

"I said the same shit; with Sin and Beretta back to themselves now, we can have everything up and running. I can't have Ahmad walking free around this bitch." My mind flashed back to this nigga saying he was Breeze's father and my blood began to boil. Ebony was foul but, fuck, I never expected her to hit a nigga where it hurts. Breeze was my fucking heart and she wasn't even my blood. I didn't need to test her to know that; Sin confirmed the shit. She pointed out that Breeze and Noelle shared the same birthmark that bitch ass nigga Ahmad had. Fuck what he was talking about; Noelle and Breeze were my fucking daughters and I'm killing everything on sight behind them.

"For your sake or Sin's?" Streetz asked, pulling me from my thoughts.

38

"What was that?" I asked confused

"You can't have him walking around for your sake or Sin's?"

"Keeping it a hundred with ya, it's for both of our comfort. I can't have my wife looking over her shoulders with every turn and I can't handle this nigga claiming my kids, so fuck him; it's headshots when I do finally catch up to him," I said as he nodded, letting me know he understood.

"You keep using that wife word, but yo ass ain't making it to the alter if Sin gets proof that your ass wanna be on your creep squad shit. On some for real shit, she ain't like these other bitches, son. And all it took to get her, you sitting here ready to throw it out. I ain't understanding that shit. You was supposed to do a solid and hold her down while she dealt with her sister. This right here ain't even you; this some disloyal shit. She held your shorty down from day one. Ain't too many females about to love your seed like they love their own."

"Yeah nigga, I hear you; who the fuck side you on anyway?" I grilled his ass.

"Alright, don't say shit else to me about the chick you creeping with. She better take my spot as pallbearer cause I ain't carrying yo ass." He cracked up and the nigga had me thinking. Sin was real life crazy and a nigga wasn't trying to die. With Blessing up now, it would be a matter of time before shit was back normal, so I needed to handle my situation. I looked up as our team started spilling in the warehouse.

"I'm going dead this lil situation before Sin have a nigga sleeping with his finger on the trigger. Let me know what ya'll come up with." I dabbed Ghost up and stood to leave.

"Aye ya'll, show him some love while he's here because Sin goin kill his ass. Don't ask why; just ask that nigga what picture he wants you to use on his rest in peace shirt," Streetz said as everyone filed in and started laughing. Chucking the deuce, I headed over to the broad I had been kicking it with house. I wasn't even trying to plan my own funeral. Everyone laughed and thought Streetz was playing but, to be honest, he wasn't lying. He was the only nigga that knew first hand that these sisters didn't fucking play. I don't know why I put myself in this water, but I definitely was making sure that I didn't drown. Pulling up, I made sure I turned my phone off; Sinaya wasn't above tracking a nigga's phone, but she was so cold that I felt like she didn't even care at this point. Walking in, the aroma of food hit me at the door.

"Damn Ghost, you scared the shit out of me. I didn't expect to see you here; why didn't you call?" she asked, holding her chest as she quickly fastened her robe. For what, I don't know because I had seen it all then some.

"Shit, I never called before; you have company?" I asked, not caring one way or the other; she wasn't my bitch.

"Now, you know I would never disrespect you like that; ain't no other nigga laying up in my spot but you."

"I guarantee you, I would not feel disrespected; only my woman could disrespect me by having another man laid up in the spot."

"What you aren't going to do is disrespect me, nigga! Sit down; let me fix you some food," she said, swaying to the kitchen. See, that's that shit I'm talking about. Sinaya was shitting on lil mama on one of her bad days, but this shit right here was what had me fucking up in the first place.

"Aye, this is the last time I'm goin fall through shawty. My girl is starting to ask questions that I don't even have an answer for. I should put my foot in your ass because you had me out until 3 in the fucking morning, turning off my alarm." I sat back, rolling me a blunt before I realized she wasn't back yet. "Yo, where the fuck the food at and what's taking you so long?" I asked, as she strolled in with a plate of country style ribs, rice, and corn; a meal I told her was my favorite. I grabbed it and the glass of soda she handed me. "You heard what I said?"

"Yeah Ghost, I knew this wouldn't last forever; just let me taste it one last time," she basically moaned. My dick jumped, but I would control him because I was beating Sinaya home, so I could fix shit. Killing the cup of soda, I started shaking my head as she went to refill it.

"Nah ma, the last time was the last time." I knew I fucked up because I had some type of feelings for her for being there for me when Sinaya neglected her duties. Fuck what Streetz was talking; a nigga was out her naked for real. Coming over here every day led to us talking and I found out it was more to her then I first thought. She was dealt a bad hand and was getting it the best way she knew how. I actually applauded her for not folding. I looked up as she made her way towards me and climbed on the table in front of my plate, then slipped two fingers in her dripping wet pussy. "The fuck is you doing?" I asked as my man got involuntarily hard.

"You don't want to fuck me, so I'll fuck myself while you eat," she said, sucking on a gold dildo like she was expecting it to bust in her mouth. She then pulled it out her mouth and slid it in her dripping wet pussy. I kid you not; the noises her pussy was making had a nigga ready to bust and it didn't help that, after only a few strokes, she made herself squirt and that shit landed in my plate. I didn't even realize I pulled out my dick and started beating it until she pushed my plate aside and her big lips clasped around my dick, as her warm throat welcomed my dick. "That ecstasy pill has your ass gone huh." I couldn't even be mad that she pulled that one on me because we had been popping them lately. Anytime I wanted to fuck her, Sin would pop up in my head and my shit wouldn't even get hard unless I popped a pill. The last time we popped one I had come over drunk, and I don't even remember much from that night except we fucked for about six hours straight. My dick felt like I was about to explode, so I grabbed her off the table and rammed her on my dick. Instead of screaming out like most bitches who couldn't take my dick, she welcomed it with a moan and started riding my dick nice and slow. When I felt her pussy muscles squeeze on my dick, a nigga moaned out like a bitch. Grabbing her waist, I started slamming her on my dick the way she liked it and the feeling of her nutting on my dick caused a nigga to almost bust. Standing up, I placed her on the kitchen table ready to shove my dick in her warm pussy, then cursed myself when I realized I went in her raw.

"Don't even trip; you can't get me pregnant twice. It's already too late." When those words crossed her lips, my dick went as soft as a punk in lesbian porno.

"The fuck you just said?" I looked at that bitch with fire in my eyes. I just know I was hearing wrong and she was just sitting here with that dick look on her face, so I repeated myself. "Peaches, the fuck you just said?"

Chapter 6

Peaches

First of all, I knew everyone was so team Ghost and Sin, but Peaches never gave a motherfuck what the next bitch thought. I already knew what everyone was thinking; she's a hoe, she's a homewrecker, lonely bitch, whatever. I'd take all that, as long as Ghost was a part of the package. Truth was, ya'll been had an opinion formed about me and I was not in the business of convincing you otherwise so, whatever you think of me, I'd go with that. Ghost could pop that fly shit about not wanting me all he wanted, but we knew what was really hood. He couldn't get enough of his peach flavored pussy, and I kept it warm and ready to serve on a silver platter. That night he embarrassed me at the club, I was done with him; well, I wanted to be done with him, but the heart wants what it wants. I had even tried to move on and started messing with a baller from out of town who was nice enough; he just wasn't Ghost.

I was far from a virgin and had my fair share of men but never one in Ghost's league. That man was cut from a cloth that was discontinued ages ago. If God took five minutes to create man, I was more than sure that he took twenty-five on Ghost. I was not speaking on just the physical attributes that he possessed either but, truth be told, that man was something special. When he walked in a room, you had no choice but to notice because everything about him screamed, "I am that nigga." He made a bitch want to sing like Kehlani; it's the way you walk, the way you talk babe, it's the way you love, the way you fuck, the way. You could say I was exaggerating all you wanted, but you ain't never had thug loving like what that nigga was serving. His bitch really fucked up when she slipped on her womanly duties and, like the boss bitch I was, I was able to luck up. Like I said, Ghost was in a league of his own, so someone better tell Sin that Peaches said game on, and I was playing for keeps.

Ghost and I had met the first day he stepped foot in Cali and that was also when my infatuation grew. If you let him tell it, the only woman he loved and would ever love was Sin, but the lie detector determined that was a lie. You know how most people have that heartfelt love at first sight story? Well, that damn sure was how I felt, although Ghost's thug ass was mean as fuck to me.

Walking in the club, all eyes was on me and I lived for that shit. I knew I was shutting shit down. My cat suit had my voluptuous curves on full display and the knee-high lace boots had my legs looking like they were going on for miles. My home girls were killing shit in the dressing department but that was it; they weren't much to look at. Janelle was half-black and Puerto Rican and had a real bad shape, one to rival Jennifer Lopez, but she was a struggle face with eyes that cocked like a pistol. Then you had Lorrie, who had the face of a model and the body of a bean bag chair that was losing some of the Styrofoam beans. Shit, I didn't care because that just put all the attention on me when we were together. You call it being a bad friend; I call it strategy. It's always chess, never checkers baby.

We made our way to our section in VIP; even though I barely had coins for my rent this month. I'll be damned if we were on the regular level. Don't judge me; there is a method to my madness. You see, I could pocket the money from the section and the bottles, but I've learned that it takes money to make money. If I stayed in the regular area, I would be around the regular niggas, and the ballers would be in the VIP section where their eyes were on the women in the sections surrounding them. No nigga wanted a woman he had to upgrade. Of course, I was looking for the upgrade, but he wouldn't do that until I put my pretty pussy on him and had him hooked on Peaches. That lesson was free; I'll have to charge for the next. The section next to us were full of niggas and, when I looked over, all I saw was grills, red bottom sneakers, bottles with the sparkles and, more importantly, cash being thrown around. I quickly plotted in my head and had my eyes on the cute mixed guy with dreads who seemed to be staring dead at me. Like God was giving me the green light, the DJ dropped my song.

Ass fat, yea I know

You just got cash, blow some mo'

Blow some mo', blow some mo'

The more you spend it, the faster it go

Bad bitches, on the floor, its rainin' hunnids

Throw some mo', throw some mo'

Throw some mo', throw some mo'

Throw some mo'

I had made it to the middle of the floor that was in the VIP area and it wasn't long before I owned that bitch. I was popping my ass and dropping it so low that the top of my ass was peeking from the low dip that the jumpsuit was cut into. If I couldn't do anything else, I could dance; after all, that was how I made my way through school. I was fucking it up when I felt the familiar feeling of money being poured over my body. Without opening my eyes, I stood up, making my ass clap as the dread head grinded behind me. He smelled so good and I instantly creamed from the familiar scent of the Gucci Guilty. With my ass on his dick, I shook my ass as I felt him waking up behind me and reached for the back of his head. I was brought back to reality when I felt waves, instead of the soft hair that I was expecting. Spinning around, my eyes fell on the ugliest motherfucker I had ever seen. I mean, this nigga made my pussy go Sahara Desert dry. Then, his ass had the nerves to smile and grab my waist. Looking over at the area where the cutie was, I noticed him and his boys cracking up and egging the man on.

"You too fine to be partying alone; you and your girls come chill with me and my niggas in my section," he demanded.

"Oh, that's your section?" I asked with my mind moving in overdrive now. I quickly looked at the floor, remembering the money he dropped on me, and my eyes bulged seeing Ben Frank so many times.

"Hell yeah, what you take me for, a stunting ass nigga? Grab your girls and come through after you gather your money." He motioned towards the floor.

"I wish the fuck I would pick that up; I ain't hurting over that change. My shoes costs more than that; as a matter of fact, give me a moment and I'll shower you with money," I lied, motioning towards these $30 boots I got from some Instagram boutique. "I'll see if my homegirls want it though." I had to boss up on him cause niggas can't stand a desperate bitch.

"Yeah, I hear you. Don't make me wait too long though; I am very impatient," he said as he walked back over to his section where everyone started laughing. Not paying it any mind, I put on the sexiest strut I could muster and made my way over to my girls.

"Aye, let's go over in that section. Before we go, grab that money off the floor and hold it until after the club. I'll split it with ya'll," I said and walked over to the section, as they headed towards the floor. My eyes connected with cutie with the dreads again, just as lil ugly walked over.

"Streetz, you my man a hundred grand and all that good shit, but shawty is mine. I told you I had three bad bitches joining us, so pick from the other two," his blocking ass said while wrapping his arms around my waist, causing my face to involuntarily frown up as my girls walked up.

"Oh shit, they must have gotten lost on the way here," the dude they called Streetz said, drawing laughs from everyone in the section.

"Don't laugh too hard like you wasn't just staring at me nigga, ole fake ass Sean Paul," I said, pissed off that he just played me in front of all these ballers. I didn't even want his ass anymore.

"Bitch, I wish the fuck I was staring at you. I was trying to remember if it was Halloween since ya'll brought out those fucking costumes," he said, drawing more laughs. Embarrassed, I walked over to the bottles and went to grab a bottle of Cîroc to pour myself a drink until I spotted a couple of bottles of Ace of Spades. I wanted to sample some for a while now, but a bitch wasn't coming off of all that money for a bottle that would do the same as some vodka, get me drunk. Before I could grab the bottle, his voice boomed over the music.

"Nah, this ain't that; take your ass back over there to the cheap liquor. Don't try to upgrade off my dime because I ain't getting shit from your bird ass." I don't know how I never noticed him before; maybe it was the fact the he was playing the back while everyone else turnt up, or I was so busy staring at Streetz. All I know is that it was then that I fell in love with Ghost something serious. It was something about a nigga that made me work for his attention, that made my pussy go drip drop. Noticing the attire he was wearing cost at least triple my rent, I bent forward and bit my bottom lip before responding.

"We can change that if you like," I said with my million-dollar smile gracing my face. Then, he said the words that changed everything for us.

"Shit, what that mouth do then?" That night, I gave him the best head of his life, and that nigga bust in my face and left the club, alone. I wound up going home with Snake after taking all the money that my friends had picked up. Fuck them, I twerked for that money. I put them in the position to be around ballers, so they should have fucking capitalized off that shit.

"The fuck you just said?" his voice boomed, pulling me back from memory lane. I didn't mean to tell him I was pregnant this way but fuck it, what's done was done. Besides, it pissed me off that his ass would notice that Sin had a new pair of shoes on but didn't realize the pudge I had. I mean, he did tell me once that I was picking up weight, but that was all he said.

"I said, it's too late for that. I'm already carrying your seed and, I don't care how much money you offer, I'm going to keep my baby," I said back up as his eyes narrowed.

"I'm glad you didn't plan on accepting money from me because I wasn't giving your bitch ass anything. I have two fucking children and I can guarantee that it ain't with your stanking ass. Bitch, I never went in you raw; you never even tasted the dick raw," he said, buttoning his pants back.

"You can pop that shit all you want Ghost, but you ain't leaving me and my baby out here naked like I'm some kind of hoe. It was me who had your back while that bitch decided to be fucking Kill Bill. I listened to you complain, fed, sucked, and fucked your ass on demand with no complaints. You can act like you forgot when you came here drunk without condoms all you want to. I'll be damned if you and that bitch live happily ever after. Play with it if you want to Ghost, I swear on our child I'll-"

"Bitch, you goin do what? The fuck you mean you ain't a hoe; what's my real name?" he asked, choking me and slamming my back against the wall. "Don't you ever in your fucking life think about threatening me again. I've killed niggas for looking in my direction with hate in their eyes, so you aren't any better if you ask me, bitch. Keep that bastard bitch or abort it if you want to because that ain't my motherfucking seed," he said, dropping me to the ground as I fought to catch my breath and stop the tears from falling. I flinched as he crossed over me and headed towards the door. "Don't try to contact me again Peaches; it would be in your best interest to forget you ever met a Ghost. As a matter of fact, if you see ghosts for Halloween, bitch, look the other way," he said, slamming my door. That's fine though; I wouldn't contact him again. He would come to me. First step was telling him; second step was telling Sin. I had his real child, so she could fall back. I know I was asking for trouble, but a bitch wasn't scared of anything and I was dickmatized. Like I said, I was playing for keeps.

Chapter 7

Blessing

The look on Sin's face when I asked about my daughter almost made my heart stop beating. I knew there was a chance she hadn't made it, but why the fuck would the doctor tell me that Sin left with my child?

"Sinaya, I can handle it; where is my baby?" I asked, fighting for the tears to stay at bay.

"Noah is with the nurses," Breeze answered, never looking up from her tablet.

"Noah? I had a son?" I asked, smiling at Sin. I had secretly wanted a little Juelz but was content when I found out I had a daughter. Sin and I argued over her name for hours and settled on Neema. I loved the meaning and it was truly a beautiful name. Looking into Sin's eyes and noticing that she was crying shocked me. This was the second time today I had seen her drop tears and that's more than I'd seen our whole life.

"Mama, please don't cry; you said Neema was okay because she was with the angels and God," Noelle said as Breeze wiped Sin's tears. I smiled at their affection; she was those girls' world and vice versa. I was going to comment on that until I noticed what Noelle had just said.

"Sinaya, what is she talking about? The doctor said you took my child home." I looked at her confused.

"You were pregnant with twins; Noah was hiding behind Neema." I felt the tears rolling down my cheeks, but I couldn't find the strength to wipe them away. "When you were shot, Neema didn't make it but Noah did. He's here, if you would like to finally meet your baby boy. I bring him every day and lay him on you, so he's very familiar with you," she said as I sat frozen. I really didn't know how to take the news. My emotions were everywhere. I was happy about my son and, of course, I was hurt because I would never know my Neema.

"Sin, I don't remember much of what happened that day; who shot me?"

"It was Emmanuel; I went get the tapes after the cops cleared out. Good thing Annette made me set up her camera's before she moved in; it helped me catch her snake ass," she said, getting so pissed that her eyes were pitch black.

"Why are you calling mom a snake? Where is she?" I asked confused.

"That bitch isn't your mom; we don't have a mother. Emmanuel was her father and, from what I gathered from the tapes, we were supposed to be dead ages ago; that bitch was supposed to kill us. Emmanuel wanted your father dead and made Annette carry out the deed. Shit went left when she fell for Sincere ugly ass."

"Sin, you look just like him." I laughed at her pettiness.

"I don't look like shit. You might look like that bitch nigga, but I ain't got shit for his ass. Anyway, she wanted your daddy ugly ass and decided she wanted to get your mama out the way," she said, rolling her eyes.

"Hold up; what the fuck are you mad at our dead mama for? Ain't shit she can do to piss you off from the grave sis." I watched as her face scrunched up in a scowl briefly before she fixed it.

"Nothing at all, I'm just pissed at the situation as a whole. Excuse the dramatics but our whole fucking life was a lie. I don't know who the fuck raised or birthed me at this point," she said, sounding frustrated.

"No matter how it happened or why it happened Sinaya, Annette still took care of us and showed us unconditional love."

"Yeah because her ass basically kidnapped us, and your bitch ass parents... your bitch ass daddy basically walked the fuck away like we wasn't shit!" she yelled, scaring the girls.

"Okkkkaaaay, change the subject. Why hasn't Rock come see me yet?" I found it funny that he wasn't here because he always followed Sinaya around.

"After everything happened, he asked for some space and hasn't really been fucking with me. To be honest, besides text messages here and there, he hasn't said much to me at all," she said, looking bothered.

"You don't think he blames us for Annette, do you? I mean, after all, she was his like his mama too." I sat back in deep thought as Sin stared off into the view out of the window. I remember calling Rock to come over because shit looked suspect, so that meant he watched me and Annette getting shot. I could only imagine how fucked up he felt. Whenever he was stressed, Rock smoked more than a train, so I knew he was somewhere higher than giraffe's pussy. "Sin, do me a favor and find our brother; bring him home, so we can talk. I've taken too many loses in my life and I refuse to lose him." She looked like she wanted to object but simply nodded her head.

"So, what's up with you and Streetz?" she cleared her throat and quickly changed the subject. Anytime a conversation got too emotional, Sin would run from it; she was always like that and I don't think she would ever change.

"I'm not forcing him to be with me and I'm not pushing him away anymore. I think I love his mixed breed ass, man." I chuckled as I thought of his foolish ass.

"Not big bad ass Beretta in love huh? We are living in the last days for real," Sin cracked a joke. "Are you ready to see Noah?" she asked, studying me carefully. Sin was a protector; she was always making sure I was comfortable. Since we were young, she would stare at me until she felt for certain that I was okay in all situations. I didn't know what kind of gift it was but, when I would feel down about Celeste, our biological mother, she would know immediately and get pictures of her and then tell me stories. Just like she studied me, I knew she was holding something back from me.

"Only after you tell me what's bothering you," I said as she looked everywhere but in my eyes. It was too late for that. I saw the tears pool in her eyes, but Sin would never let them fall.

"Ghost is cheating; I have no proof but he is." She shocked me. Ghost loved the ground Sinaya walked on. I was convinced he would go to war with God behind Sin, so I didn't want to accept that.

"Sinaya, are you sure? I don't know; I would expect that from anyone other than Ghost. You two are always so happy together."

"Shit, I can't blame him; after everything happened, I checked out. I laughed at Streetz but, just the month you were gone, I think my body count rose drastically. I stopped counting after I hit ten within the first week of you being in that coma. I stopped taking care of home, hired a nanny, and stopped paying him attention. That's no excuse though because he knew what I was dealing with; he was supposed to understand what I was going through. It hurt so bad to lose you all at once. First, Annette. Right, I wanted to be sad cause she was gone, but I was so fucking angry for what she had done. Disloyalty of any form was not tolerated. But, then, I missed calling her for simple things and, after her, it was always your number I called next. Well, of course, you weren't answering anytime soon. That slowly started weighing down on me. Then Rock checking out pushed me over the edge. I had no choice but to hire a nanny. People said I didn't need help with my family but, truth be told, I couldn't look my babies in the eyes. I was afraid they would be gone next. My biggest fear is being alone, and it was becoming a reality," she said, wiping the one tear that had finally escaped, while my face was soaked with them.

"Sis-" I began but was interrupted.

"No, let me go get Noah; that's enough of this crying moment." She stood to her feet and made her way out the door in the blink of an eye. After playing with Noah, who I instantly fell in love with, and the girls, their Nanny came to pick them up and Sinaya and I talked until she started yawning.

"Sis, can I see those tapes from the house?" I gathered the courage to ask.

"No, unfortunately, they are all destroyed." She answered too quickly for me to believe. I accepted the kiss on the cheek and the hug before I laid back for a nap I felt was well needed.

Chapter 8

Sinaya

Holding secrets from Blessing wasn't easy, but she wasn't ready for the truth, at least not yet. I knew I had to tell her, but I knew my sister better than she knew herself. Blessing was too forgiving and that was where the problem lied. A part of me knew I was protecting my sister, but the other part of me knew that I wasn't willing to share her with people who I didn't believe deserved to know her. Not paying attention to where I was going, I bumped head first into a hard body, causing me to fall on my ass, hard.

"Let me find out you already falling for a young rich nigga," Rello said with a huge smile, showing off his iced out bottom grill.

"I did fall for a young rich nigga and his name is Ghost." I laughed, grabbing the hand he extended to help me off the floor. Standing to my feet, Rello stepped closer into my personal space with his arm wrapped around my waist. He sucked on his teeth before hitting my ass with the sexiest smirk I'd seen on a man. "Wh-what are you doing here?" This man had my head fucked up and I haven't ever sweat a nigga like I was sweating this one.

"Why you nervous Sin, shaking and shit; a nigga ain't going bite you." He smiled again, showing a row of perfect white teeth at the top and that damn blinged out grill at the bottom.

"Boy, I ain't stunting you; Ghost goin fuck you up if you keep playing with me though," I said, nervously laughing and looking around. Shit, don't get me wrong. I'm not scared of no nigga walking this green Earth, but I couldn't deny that Ghost seeing me hugged up with this nigga wasn't drama I needed. It didn't matter whether I thought he was cheating or not, my loyalty wouldn't be tested off of just a hunch.

"You know I ain't scared of shit Sin; that's why you sweating the kid. I respect you enough to not put you in that situation though. When you find out for sure that he's a fuck up, hit my line. I got you ma," he said, releasing my handing and pulling me in for a hug that lasted a few seconds too long to still be considered friendly. The clearing of someone's throat made me want to spin around, but the fear of it being Ghost had a bitch frozen. I was literally stuck and Rello's ass wasn't helping because he was laughing like shit was hilarious. I found my ass saying a quick prayer, then counting to three, before I stepped back. Finally back out of Rello's arms, I turned around and was met by Streetz sporting the meanest mug.

"What's up Sin?" he asked, never breaking eye contact with Rello, who was smiling big as ever. Something was wrong with his crazy ass and something had to be wrong with me because I was feeling the fuck out the worker, like I didn't have one of the bosses.

"Ain't shit, just happy my sister up. Blessing in there about to fall asleep, if you wanted to go see her before she started snoring like a grizzly bear," I said, giving him the hint to walk away.

"Oh, you spoke to Ghost yet? You remember him right? My brother, your man, father of your kids, the crazy one?" he said with his messy ass.

"Nah but, if you speak with him, see if he'll be home on time tonight, while you're sitting here trying to check something. This ain't that Streetz. I'm grown as fuck and I've been this way for a few years now. Fall back," I said, mugging him as he backed up with his hands in mock surrender. Laughing, he walked into Blessing's room and I already knew his ass was about to snitch.

"Let me find out I got you in trouble though." Rello laughed, causing me to hit his ass with the middle finger. "If you scared, I can come home with you or you with me; the choice is totally up to you," he said, no longer laughing. This nigga was nuts.

"And what will you coming home with me to supposedly do?" I had to ask.

"Shit, you can just call me Rello, the ghostbuster." He smiled. Shaking my head, I spun on my heels and hit that nigga with a deuce before he got me caught up. I knew it was going to be drama when I got home and I already had a headache.

***

A month after Streetz ass decided to snitch on the interaction between Rello and I, and Ghost was still staying out late like I was new to this. That hug was just his excuse to show his ass without feeling guilty, but what's good for him was damn sure good for me. When he was out and about, the kids were with Ms. Lee Ann and I was with Rello. We never had sex or anything because I was still being somewhat faithful to a nigga I knew was cheating.

"Sin, we have a meeting at the warehouse; you may want to carry your almost married ass home and get ready, unless you rolling up there with me," Rello said with humor in his voice, while stepping out of the shower and walking back into his massive bedroom. I involuntarily licked my lips as I watched the monster he called a dick swing from side to side. "Look at you, about to start drooling and shit. You better not slob on my fucking bed Sinaya; I told you say the word and I'll put him in your life," he said, smirking as he made his way into the closet. Standing up, I slid my Adidas crop top sweater and matching tights on over my boy shorts and bra. I was so beat from running behind the kids that I came over undressed and cuddled next to Rello for some much needed rest.

"Nah, I'm not even going. I don't feel good; I'm going get some rest," I said as he stepped out in some lightwash denim Robin jeans, a red Polo v-neck t-shirt, and a fresh pair of red Balenciaga sneakers. As usual, his haircut looked two minutes old and his waves had a bitch seasick.

"Stop looking at me like that before I fuck the curls out your head Sinaya," Rello said, walking up to me and wrapping his arms around me. Not being able to stop myself, I grabbed his bottom lip between my teeth and softly sucked on it. It always looked so succulent, so I had to see what it was hitting for. What I didn't expect was for his ass to kiss me with so much passion that my knees buckled. And his ass really let me collapse on the ground, then walked away.

61

"What the fuck Rello?" I screamed as he grabbed his wallet and keys, headed towards the door that led to the garage.

"You playing with fire ma. I'm trying to respect you, really, I am, but you almost got fucked dizzy just now. You have a key; lock up on your way out. Make sure my security gate closes all the way before you pull completely out," he said, staring me in the eyes and walking out moments before I heard his car start up. I had to head to the bathroom and take off my panties because those motherfuckers were drenched.

Heading home, I remembered I hadn't fed Kash and Dollar, and I'm sure Ghost's ass had already bypassed my condo I kept them in. It would be easier to just take them home but, for some reason, Breeze was scared of them, yet she got along great with Grim and Reaper. Busting a u-turn in the street, I headed towards my second home to feed my babies. After letting them roam free in the backyard for a few hours, I brought them in the room where their food was waiting for them. Ignoring another one of Ghost's millions of calls, I heard the doorbell ringing and just knew his ass wanted to argue; he was so careless with his keys. I screamed it was open and went back to playing with my dogs. If push came to shove and he aggravated me too much, I would feed his ass to my babies. I laughed aloud to myself but was interrupted by Kash and Dollar growling and a female's voice.

"I wasn't looking for you, but I guess I could get this out of the way." I spun around and came face to face with the female that was with Ghost in the club for my birthday. Only difference was this bitch was very much pregnant.

"Fruit salad right?" I asked with humor in my voice but none in my eyes. Making a clicking noise, I made my dogs lie down at my feet.

"Peaches, but you knew that," she said, rubbing her belly.

"Grape, orange, pear, either way it goes, your mama was wrong as fuck. So, how can I help you?" I asked with my hands on my hips. I knew as soon as I looked at her what this was about but, instead, I wanted to give my nigga the benefit of the doubt.

"Well, Ghost didn't know how to tell you, so I'm here to say it for him. I'm where he wants to be at; in a few months, we will be welcoming our child and we plan on being a family." I interrupted her with my laughter but stopped when I noticed she wasn't laughing.

"Oh, you're serious aren't you? Why hasn't he told me this then?" I entertained her.

"I don't deny that he loves you, but we are actually in love and, besides that, I did something you couldn't. I actually gave him a child cause your daughter is just that, your daughter." She laughed and everything was going fine until she mentioned my daughter. It's some unwritten law that you never mention another woman's child in no way, shape, or form. Clicking my tongue twice, Dollar and Kash stood at attention and began growling at her. The smirk fell from her face as piss trickled down her leg.

"Get the fuck in the room," I said, pulling my gun from behind my back.

"Sin, i-it's not ev-even this serious. I swear, I won't bother you anymore. Ju-just let me go pl-please," she stammered, easing her way into the room and cowering against the wall. Making another series of clicking noises, Kash and Dollar walked into the room and stood in front the door as I closed and locked it. They wouldn't touch her, yet.

"You stay still and quiet and they won't attack; you move a muscle and they will tear that ass up. And they haven't ate in days," I lied through the door.

Me: Get your ass to the condo now! You have five minutes.

Punkassniggabitch: We have a meeting.

Me: Looks like you have a decision to make, time starts now.

If I wasn't already half passed pissed, I would laugh at his new name in my phone. That had Rello's childish ass written all over it. I made my way to the bar and fixed me a couple shots of Patron. I needed that shit because no matter how much you assumed your man was cheating, nothing prepared you for the breath that gets knocked out of you when the proof was smack dab in your face. I collapsed on the couch and bit down on a throw pillow to mask the sound of the scream that escaped from my stomach. If this was what heartbreak felt like, I never wanted a heart again. I don't know how long I sat there silently crying but, when I came to my senses again, Ghost was lightly tapping me in the face and calling my name.

"Sinaya, say something to me, ma. Man, what the fuck!"

"Ghost," I whispered in a voice I didn't remember. It was void of any emotion and my heart no longer hurt in that moment. "I asked you never to hurt me; I begged you not to hurt me. I didn't want this; I don't do relationships. You forced this shit on me. Your ass was showing up at my house, showing up on my dates, and showing your ass. Nigga, you forced me in a relationship, just to fuck me over in the end."

"Sin, I know we haven't been good for a while but you know why. If you hadn't been hugged up-," was all he got before I stood up and slapped the fuck out of him. I had slapped him so hard, my hand was on fire and he had a look of shock on his face. We never put our hands on each other and here we were on the verge of calling it quits.

"Nigga, I hugged Rello. And? I never fucked him; he hasn't even smelled my pussy! Nigga couldn't tell you if I waxed, trimmed, or was a grizzly bear down there. But you, my nigga, you fucked that funky pussy bitch raw nigga!" I spat while punching him in the eye, instantly closing that shit; I quickly backed up, grabbed my gun, and pointed it at him. I was pissed off, but I wasn't stupid. I knew better than hitting a man because you open the door for them to hit your ass back; like I said, I was pissed. "Ghost, you know how I give it up love; take your charge cause you fucked up. What if you brought me something home, then what? Did yo stupid ass think that far?"

"You think I cheated on you, Red? You sound insecure as fuck," he said, holding his eye and sounding hurt. Leave it to a nigga to have you looking like the problem. That bitch wasn't lying; if I didn't know anything, I knew how to read the fuck out of someone, and she was pregnant or had the opportunity to fuck my man.

"So, you haven't fucked Peaches since we got together?" I watched as the wrinkle in his forehead formed, a sign of the lie to come.

"What? No, I ain't worried about that bitch," he spat.

"So, the child she's pregnant with can't be yours, right?" I asked as that wrinkle appeared once more.

"Shit, if she is pregnant, that's news to me. What, she told you that dumb shit and you believed her huh? You just want a reason to make you being hugged up with that nigga cool. Fuck outta here with that bullshit Red!"

"So, if I call here, ask her, and she confirms that it is your child, then what?" I asked, pacing the floor.

"Shit, then she a motherfucking lie. Even before us, I never fucked her raw." I nodded then headed to the room she was locked in, leaving Ghost in the front. Making a clicking noise, my babies stepped away from the door as Peaches stood up.

"Sin, please let me go." She cried.

"I will say this one time and one time only Peaches. I don't like liars and, now that you know, whose baby is that?" I knew it was a chance that this baby was his and that's a chance I wasn't willing to take. At the end of the day, I had too much invested in my family and I'd be damn if a bitch was sold Walt Disney dreams of a happily ever after on some shit I wasn't seeing and ending to.

"Gho-," was all she was able to say before two bullets ripped through her stomach from the end of my Beretta.

"Sinaya, what the fuck!" I heard Ghost scream before I clicked my tongue and Kash and Dollar met him in the hallway growling. "Come get these fucking dogs before I kill them; what the fuck happened?" he screamed but never came closer.

"I got rid of the possibility. You said it wasn't your child, she said it was; you both were obviously confused, so I helped her get an abortion. You shouldn't be sad; after all, it wasn't yours, right?" I smirked, walking out into the hallway and clicking my tongue for Kash and Dollar to follow.

Chapter 9

Ghost

"You heard from Sin yet?" Streetz asked, walking in the warehouse for one of our weekly meetings. I focused my attention on the bottle of Hennessey that seemed to be attached to my side since my woman decided she wanted to be a ghost this time around. A nigga ain't never had his heart broken before, but I would bet my last million that this was what that shit felt like. I fucked up and that might have cost me my woman.

"Stop asking me that shit every fucking day!" I roared at Streetz. He simply nodded his head and walked out; I knew he was trying to respect my situation because any other time, we would go toe to toe for how I just came at him. A nigga felt like shit; the look in Red's eyes when she pointed that gun at me let me know I fucked up. There wasn't a trace of love there. On top of that, her voice was void of any emotion and she killed Peaches' child with no remorse. That had me fucked up too because I knew there was a possibility that the child was mine, but I lied my ass off and it wasn't shit I could do about that. Peaches didn't die, but she couldn't stay in no fucking hospital with Sin's crazy ass on the loose. After she was rushed into surgery, I hired the doctor and some nurses to care for her at my house. I was never there any damn way and I knew I was to blame for this. Granted, no one told her stupid ass to approach Sinaya in the first fucking place. Like I said, a nigga felt like shit all around and I didn't have the slightest idea where my woman was.

A familiar scent tickled my noise and a nigga almost fell out the chair trying to see where it was coming from; it was one of Sin's scents. Turning the corner, my heart dropped when I saw it was only Beretta. I was happy as fuck that she was up and moving since the shooting, but I wanted, no, I needed her to be Sin at that very moment.

"Damn Ghost, you look like you've been stressing," she said, shaking her head at me in pity.

"I don't need your pity Beretta; my niggas have been combing the streets looking for Sin and you sitting there all nonchalant like your sister ain't missing," I snapped.

"Cause her ass ain't missing. I talk to my sister every day; in fact, the girls saw her yesterday for a few hours," she said with a smirk. "She told me to tell you to stop searching because she will only be found when she chooses to be found. She needed space."

"What the fuck you mean she needed space? Tell Sinaya bring her ass home now so we can talk like adults; she ain't a fucking child that can just run away when she feels like it!" I screamed, stepping in Beretta's face as Streetz stepped forward and pushed me back. If I was in my right mind, I would have never stepped to my boy's woman and, even if she wasn't his, I would have never stepped to her crazy ass anyway. It had been a week since Sinaya had pulled her disappearing act and no one had heard from her, outside of her sister. I watched as her eyes went black and heard guns cocking. I hadn't even noticed she had a few of her men in here with her today.

69

"Ghost, let me start off by saying, whenever you feel the need to start feeling yourself and approach me like I'm pussy, don't. Cause everyone in this bitch knows Beretta will catch more fucking bodies then a coroner over some disrespect. You fucked up when you decided to make that bitch feel like she could one up my sister. Then, she brought that to her front door Ghost. How the fuck she knew about the condo if your ass never brought her there? Truth be told, I'm shocked your ass still breathing and in one piece; I would have chopped that ass up like sushi and dropped one of your body pieces in front of every bitch you ever fucked with since middle school's door, so you could really rest in pieces." She finished staring at Streetz, who spit his water out.

"What you looking over here for? That nigga cheated, not me. Nah ma, this ain't that type of party. I'm a one crazy woman type of man; direct your attention back on him please," he said, really looking scared. I think she beats him when no one was around; there was no way a grown man should be so scared of a woman. They had made it official and, from what I saw, they damn sure doing better than my relationship was.

"I never told that hoe where Sin's place was; she never got that address from me. If it was the house, I could say she followed me on a drunken night, but not the fucking condo." I knew shit looked all bad, but why the fuck would I lead Peaches to Sin? That shit was a fuck up waiting to happen.

"So, we're finally admitting that you did sleep with Peaches? Check this Ghost; no one wanted you and Sinaya together more than

I did. I felt you made her happy. Now, I'm feeling like you don't even deserve her, son. Sinaya ain't like none of these basic bitches, so you should have never treated her like one. To be honest, you were about to be the first body I caught since the shooting, but I guess she still loves you because she told me to leave your ass alone. I had already decided that, if she looked like this affected her when I saw her yesterday though, you were a dead man walking. I guess that other nigga took her mind off of shit," she said before walking out the door. It took me a moment to register what she just said and I tried to run behind her, but her men blocked the door and so did Streetz.

"Aye, you fucked up. Walk it off, but you won't be approaching my woman about nothing she said." He stared me in my eyes to let me know he meant business.

"Man fuck!" I screamed, throwing the bottle of liquor against the wall.

"Find my fucking wife!" I screamed at all the men in the room before walking to the back office and slamming the door. A nigga could dish out a lot of shit, but I knew Sin better not be with some nigga. Behind my wife, the city was going to bleed until she brought her ass home. Sin had a nigga stressing man. Blessing had to be lying; my bitch was somewhere hurting, but she wasn't with no nigga.

Chapter 10

Rello

"Sin, I ain't going on another motherfucking ride, that shit lame." I laughed as she ran around like a big ass child. What I didn't expect when she left my house the other night was for her and those two big ass grizzly bears to be sitting in my house in the dark, drinking hot cocoa and shit. I could tell something went down, but she didn't want to speak and I was not going to force her.

"If you're scared, say you scared Rello!" she clowned as she headed towards another ride. Yesterday, she told me she needed a break from Cali, so we flew out to Texas and her ass dragged me to Six Flags. While it was good to see a genuine smile on her face, baby girl had me all kinds of fucked up. I could fight and shoot my way out of anything, but a nigga can't walk away unharmed from falling off one of these big ass rides. I watched the news and that shit happened every day.

"Yeah alright, if your big water head ass fall and hit the ground, I'm flying back home like I wasn't with you and I'll even hold Beretta as she cries for you," I said with no smile.

"Nigga, you would leave me?" she asked, cracking up.

"Fucking right, Beretta ain't shooting me. I heard about her crazy ass. You're on your own!" I said, lifting her in the air as she screamed, making everyone stare our way. "Aye, stop all that fucking noise, like you ain't out here cheating," I said, slapping her on her ass.

72

"Rello, ain't nobody cheating with you." She laughed.

"Shit, you was thinking about it; I saw how you were watching a nigga get dressed earlier. You was wishing this dick was rearranging organs like a waist trainer."

"If I wanted to fuck, I would say 'Rello, I want to fuck'," she said as I put her on her feet.

"Yeah, I hear you; let's go back to the room. I need to shower and get dressed. I'm starving." We made our way back to the parking lot and grabbed a shuttle walking hand in hand. I knew Sin was in love with Ghost and that she was going back to him but fuck it; she was mine for the moment. I ain't no sucker for love ass nigga neither, so cancel that thought. Sin was a breed of her own and her man didn't appreciate that shit. I saw him a few times with that bitch, Peaches, and knew he was living foul, but I didn't speak on other men. Like my nigga Gates said, that's irregular. When the story was told to me, all I could do was shake my head at Ghost's clown ass. He let Peaches' hoe ass ruin what he had with Red and she had already told my homeboy the baby was his too. Oh well, his fuck up and I'm capitalizing.

Following Sin to the room, I couldn't keep my eyes off of her ass. Being that we were in the sun all day, she was dressed in a pair of white denim shorts that she knew her ass was way too thick for. They just barely covered her ass and her thick thighs spilled out of them in the sexiest of ways. Her swag was on point, as usual, and she wore a crop top Heat jersey and a pair of Flu games on her feet.

With every step she took, I watched as her ass jiggled and I had to adjust my dick.

"I'm about to hop in the shower first," she quickly said as she ran to the bathroom and got the water started. Her bald ass knew I said I was going shower. I watched as she went to her luggage and began looking for clothes to wear and made my way to the bathroom. "Rello, what you about to do cause I know you heard me?" she said with her hands on her hips.

"Well damn, can I take a piss before you hog up the bathroom?" I playfully mugged her then walked in the bathroom, where I stripped and hopped in her shower water. I didn't know who the fuck she thought I was, but she was going to learn today. God punished my ass because the water almost burned my fucking skin. What's wrong with females; they act like they're allergic to cold water or some shit? Adjusting the water, I couldn't help but to think about Sin's fine ass being in the next room and my dick grew harder again; I couldn't have her yet, so I beat my dick like a man. Just as I was about to nut, the shower curtain flew open and Sin was standing there ass naked.

"Remember when I said if I wanted to fuck, I would say 'Rello, I want to fuck'?" she asked, staring at my dick and biting her lip. "Well Rello, I want to fuck." She stepped in the bathtub and dropped to her knees under the stream of the water, swallowed my dick whole. I ain't one to brag, but my dick was impressive; bitches couldn't take the width alone and here she was swallowing me like my shit was tiny. It didn't take me long before my toes started curling and I needed to nut, so I attempted to move her head, but she hit my hands and swallowed my seeds. Standing to her feet, she smirked, stepped out of the tub, and grabbed a towel to wrap around her body. "Now that the first one is out the way, there should be no reason why you can't last all night, right?" she asked over her shoulder, as she headed to the bedroom. A nigga almost bust his ass trying to get out that shower as fast as I could. Fuck a towel, I stepped out that bitch dick swinging and water dripping. If my dick wasn't already hard, Sin lying at the edge of the bed playing with her pussy had it on brick. I watched for a second as her juices coated her fingers and she threw her head back on the verge of cumming, but I couldn't have that. I quickly stepped forward, moved her hand, and filled her up with my dick. Between the moans she was making, how wet she was, and the fact that her pussy was tighter than Shaq in a Honda coupe, a nigga had to think of stupid shit to stop myself from nutting up. With every stroke, I felt her pussy muscles choking my dick. Looking down and seeing her juices coating it made me start digging deeper into her pussy.

"Fuuuuccccckkkk Rello, what are you doooinnnggg to meeeee!" she screamed while grabbing two handfuls of her hair. I laughed as she began trying to back paddle to the headboard and gripped her waist.

"Nah, you Sin bad ass huh; take this dick. You don't run from shit, so don't run now," I said, lifting her up with my dick still inside of her. I fell back on the bed, so she could ride. Placing her feet firmly on the bed, she smirked then took me on the ride of my life. A nigga turned straight bitch with all the moaning I was doing; Sin had my toes curling and she had never looked sexier than she did at that moment. With her eyes closed and her hair falling all over her face, I could tell she was concentrating on busting this nut, so I started pulling her down by her waist and pushing my dick deep into her wet pussy. That didn't last long because as soon as she started squirting on my dick, I followed with the biggest nut I ever busted. That shit took all my energy and she must have agreed because I heard her softly snoring with my dick still inside of her.

Watching her sleep, I knew I was playing with fire. A nigga ain't stupid; I knew, although he fucked up, her heart remained with that fuck nigga Ghost. I had nothing personal against him, besides the fact that he had what I wanted. Women like Sinaya weren't created every day. I knew she would wake up feeling some kind of way about what happened because she would feel like her loyalty was questioned. She was hurting, so I fucked her into a quick healing. Just as I was thinking of maybe telling her let's keep shit on a friendly level for her sake, I felt her pussy getting wet around my dick and she woke the beast up. Being a gentleman, I attempted to lift her up and let her sleep until she started grinding her hips against me. That was the beginning of a very long night. I'm far from pussy, so Ghost would never hear of this from my mouth but, after the dick down she just got, her ass would be back. And I would dick her down each and every time.

"What the fuck did I do?" she asked herself after what had to be the sixth round.

"Raped me," I answered with a serious voice.

"He cheated on me, got the bitch pregnant, and all. He was supposed to understand why I wasn't myself for a while. I was losing everything that meant something to me. Can you believe she was pregnant for my man and had the nerves to show up at my doorstep to tell me they were going to be a family?" she whispered.

"Was pregnant?" I asked, catching the past tense she used.

"Shit, he said it wasn't his and she claimed it was; I didn't want her to have that poor baby confused, so I got rid of it," she said nonchalantly.

"Man, you real life nuts. Nah but, on some real shit, don't sit here beating yourself up. You're faithful to that nigga 24/7 and look where that got you. Ma, I ain't about to sit here and tell you to leave that nigga because he can love you differently than I can. I ain't on that shit right now. I'm a young, rich nigga just looking to get his dick wet from time to time. So, if you ever need someone to put the pussy on, then you still have my keys and my numbers. Don't sit here on some you fucked up shit though; you just evened the playing field. Now, ya'll can start to move on. Aye, he gotta love you anyway; I saw that black eye you gave son. Couldn't have been me because I would have shot you in your eye."

"How you take my virginity then tell me you ain't looking for love nigga?" She looked at me with a serious face until we both bust out laughing.

"Shut dha fuck up bruh, like you don't have a whole kid out here. And you damn sure didn't fuck me like a virgin. Matter of fact, before you go back to being that nigga's ride or die, hop on this dick again. Put on one of my chains and throw it to the back like Pinky used to do before she went dumb on the dick." I laughed until her ass got up to really go another round. "Aww no, I was joking; I ain't no machine ma. My dick sensitive as fuck right now; leave it alone for a few hours witcho nympho ass."

"Man, you for real? I ain't have no dick in about two months, man," she pouted.

"Better go holla at your man; the sausage shop closed for repair. Matter of fact, watch out so I can go put some boxers on; you staring at my man like you really going rape me. I don't play cops, but I will send your ass straight to jail, don't pass go, or collect $200," I said, dodging the pillow she threw my way.

"This ain't rape, it's consensual."

"You a black ass lie. I watch Law and Order: Special Victims Unit, no means no, Sinaya!" I cracked up as she laid against me and dozed off. I popped all the shit about not wanting to be in love and that was all a lie. I wanted Sin in the worst way and, if Ghost decided to kick the bucket today, I would be proposing to Sin before the body had time to cool off. The thing was, I ain't the nigga that's going to cause complications in her life. I loved her that much.

78

Chapter 11

Sinaya

"Your ass would just stroll in here dressed like a damn ghost after being missing for two weeks huh," Blessing joked as I bounced into the warehouse for an impromptu meeting Ghost threw together. He didn't know I was back and that's just how I wanted it.

"Well, I was feeling a lil Godly when I selected this," I said, referring to the all-white jumpsuit I was rocking. Although it had a plunging neckline, it wasn't too revealing and, even with the loose fit I was going for with the wide legs, it still clung to my curves like a baby to its mama. I kept it simple with gold accessories and a pair of gold Gucci flats, just in case Ghost decided to jump stupid because of my disappearing act.

"Yeah, I hear ya, let me give you a lil warning. That nigga looks a mess; he needs a shower, a retwist, a barber, and probably a new liver because his ass is best friends with every bottle of liquor he sees. Ya'll need to shake back because the girls definitely notice and have been asking if you were mad at them," she finished, never looking up from her phone.

"I'm good, now. I think I'm gonna go back to the therapist. Everything that's been happening has really turned me into a person I don't know. I'm so angry and I haven't been around the girls because I don't wanna snap on them. We'll be good though, and he'll shake back because I'm going back home after this meeting. Are you even listening to me? Who are you over there texting anyway?" I asked, looking over her shoulder and reading the text. "I know you didn't tell them where the fuck our warehouse is located Blessing!" I snapped when I saw her, Young, and Sunjai in a group message.

"I know how you feel about them, but I trust them. So, we are all going to have a talk and, if it doesn't solve anything, we can walk away and never speak to them again. You know I wouldn't go against you; my loyalty lies here," she finished as the team crawled in and walked over to show me love. My team had always been like a family to me, so going so long without being here made me feel some type of way. I really needed to get my life back in sync.

"Tech, let me holla at you," I said, once Tech made his way in the building.

"Wassup Sin, glad to see you're back." He smiled. Tech was a very attractive man. Standing at 6'1", he put you in the mind of Lance Gross. Fine as he was, even if there was no Ghost, I would never date Tech. The reason his ass was around was because he could find anybody, anywhere! I feel sorry for the woman who ends up with him; she better be a real life Ayesha Curry or his ass would know.

"What's going on with the search for my brother?" We had been looking for Rock for a while and the shit was driving me nuts that he would just disappear.

"Sin, he hasn't left a paper trail anywhere. I've been looking too; you know he's a brother to me too."

"Yeah, I know and I appreciate it; don't stop looking. He will pop up soon," I said, willing it to happen. At first, I wanted to believe he just needed some time to deal with everything going on. Thinking about it now, Rock would have called, even if to tell me he was okay. Everything in me was screaming that we had a problem and I was beginning to worry. I didn't care what I had going on in my life, I was going to make sure my brother was found.

"Look who decided to grace us with her presence." Streetz came over and gave me a hug. "Maybe now that nigga will let us have a life outside of finding Waldo. Hell, I can't even enjoy my woman being home because that nigga has us searching for you like you is Osama Bin Laden ass." He cracked as Ghost walked in, looking like a shadow of the man that I loved.

What I admired about Ghost was he was a fucking boss and, when he walked in a room, you had no choice but to know that; this man in front of me wasn't my man. I watched as he sniffed in the air and his eyes scanned everyone's faces until they landed on mine. I smiled when his whole demeanor changed; his shoulders really lifted, like weight was removed from them. That's the shit that had me stuck; that man knew everything about me down to my scent. I thought the bond we shared was comparable to none, so I couldn't front like I wasn't still bothered by his cheating. No woman wanted to know that another woman could so easily take something you worked hard to put together. It made you feel like all you did was a waste. Despite all of that, the heart wants what it wants, as I was drawn to Ghost like a moth to a flame. I made my way to him, and he pulled me in for a hug and just exhaled.

"Sinaya look-" he began with his mouth to my ear.

"We will talk when we get home," I whispered in his ear before taking my seat at the table with him by my side. For the duration of the meeting, my mind was on the sit down with Blessing and her family because they damn sure were not mine, which was to follow.

"You need me to stay with you?" Ghost asked as everyone filed out of the warehouse once the meeting came to an end.

"Nope, this will be quick and easy. I'm heading to my house after this, so we will talk about our situation then," I said, but it was pointless because the guests of honor had already arrived. Standing to my feet, I thanked God I was wearing flats as I quickly crossed the room. I noticed Streetz and Blessing shaking their head before I stood in front of Aimee.

"Is there something wrong?" she asked with a mug on her face.

"Nah, remember in the hospital when I told you whenever I caught you without my kids it would be on site. I don't know what that means where you come from but, around here, that means no talking, so I'm sparing you at the moment. My children ain't here and this is the next time I saw you." I knew she was coward because instead of swinging, her ass went to cover her face, so I changed my mind and didn't knock her ass out like I planned too; but I did slap the fuck out of her a few times for disrespecting me twice, before I felt hands pulling me back. Spinning around, I threw a quick two-piece at Young, who was able to side step the first but that second one connected with his jaw and put him on his ass. "Fuck is wrong with your ass, touching me while I'm trying to show her ass some manners? Nigga, who the fuck told you touching me was a good idea at all?" I spat at him.

"Didn't I tell his ass not to touch her?" I heard Ghost say to Blessing before she burst out laughing.

"Young, how the fuck you and Aimee both get beat up by your big sister? Sin, I know you aren't fucking with me at the moment or whatever but, next time he try to boss up on me, can I give you a call? You don't even have to talk to me; I'll use a keyword. I'll just be like clean up on aisle three," Sunjai said, causing everyone to laugh but Aimee and Young, who were mugging me. Just as I was about to ask if something was wrong, I was interrupted.

"If you didn't already look like me, that would be the proof I needed that you were my daughter," Sincere's bitch ass said, smiling like a proud father.

"Nigga, I ain't shit to you, so you can wipe that smile from your face; my daddy died, along with my mother," I said, walking over to help Young up from the floor. "I won't apologize for rocking your ass cause I ain't sorry; you need to either teach her some manners or put a muzzle on her ass. How the fuck she talks so much shit but can't fight?" I said, referring to Aimee, who had found her way behind Sincere and, I swear, if looks could kill, I would be dead. "Don't fucking look at me like that's going place fear in my heart."

"I'll give you that bi-" Aimee started before I cut her off from making a mistake.

"There you go with that word again; bitch, I will shoot his ass just to get to you. You have a whole lot of heart for a weak hoe. You ain't giving me shit; I took that!" I spat.

"Blessing, maybe we should reschedule this for when she's in a better mood. I know that I fucked up Sinaya and I can understand your anger, but what you won't do is talk to me like I'm pussy. You may not have heard of me but do your research," Sincere said, standing to his feet to leave.

"Whether you leave or stay makes no difference to me, but understand this. I won't be in attendance for another dysfunctional ass family meeting. And don't tell me do my research like I don't know everything, and I do mean every detail, about your ass. So, let's talk; ain't that what you came for?" I asked, sitting again and crossing my legs. "Young, please escort Aimee ass out of my fucking building because if she keeps looking at me like she can beat me, I will test that theory, and I ain't talking any bitch ass slaps either," I said, not even bothering to look her way. "So, Sincere, let's talk. I have a few questions and I'm sure you have some of your own."

"Regardless of how you feel about me, I'm proud of you girls. The moves you make and the ability to stay under the fed's radar while doing so is impressive. I hope you can at least build a bond with your brother and sister; they did nothing," he pleaded.

"Anyway," I dismissed that theory, "I know what sparked everything but, if you are big bad Sin, why did you stay gone so long?"

"So, you know everything about Annette?" he asked.

"I know probably more than you know, but we will get to that shortly. Can you go ahead and answer the question please?"

"Well, let me start from the beginning because I owe everyone this explanation; I haven't even told this story to Sunjai and Young, so excuse them for not understanding your anger towards me. When we first met Annette, Celeste was pregnant with Blessing and we all worked at University hospital. I didn't like or trust Annette from the jump because she always slithered too much for me. She would show up at the house when she knew Celeste was scheduled to be at work, wearing the least amount of clothes possible, or I would always catch her staring at Celeste with so much hatred in her eyes. I tried to warn Celeste, but she would just tell me I was overreacting and I didn't like anyone. She thought Annette was her first real friend; that was her problem. Back then, she was too trusting, always wanted to see the good in people.

When she went into labor, I begged her not to let Annette in the room, but she said Anette was Blessing's god mother and she promised to let her name her. Everything was going well until it wasn't. I took my eyes off of Annette for a few moments to cut the umbilical cord and that was all she needed to inject her with the drugs that slowed her heart rate. Everyone was so focused on Blessing that they didn't notice Celeste until it was too late. I knew it was Annette; when our eyes connected, she wore a smirk. In the weeks to follow, I wouldn't allow her in my home or near Blessing or Sinaya, and she didn't handle that well. What no one knew was your mom and I was deeply involved in the drug game. It was passed down from my father and I accepted the throne. Furthering my education simply helped me get my hand on any drug I could think of, legally in a way.

My pops never had a problem with the feds in his business and neither did I until Annette turned informant. Hell hath no fury like a woman scorned. The hit she put on me and the feds breathing down my neck I could handle, had it not been for you two. I couldn't put your lives in jeopardy. So, I left you where I knew you would be safe, with her. There wasn't a doubt in my mind that she loved you girls. I knew of what happened to her back in Haiti, so I knew she would cherish you girls. I left everything behind and started over," he finished.

"So, what made you come back all these years later?" I asked.

"The scare of the feds was gone and we were going to kill Annette and Emmanuel; I didn't know there was someone more ruthless then me out there though." He winked at me.

"One more question, Sunjai and Young, who is your mother?" I asked, smiling at my father.

"No, don't put them in this; all questions will be directed towards me!" he roared.

"What's going on?" Blessing asked.

"Well, fuck, I figured since this is a family meeting, why the fuck isn't the whole family present? What you didn't know, Sincere, is that each of our homes is equipped with high definition cameras." I watched the color drain from his face and my smile widened. "After my mom was killed and my sister shot, I got to thinking. When Rock called me, he kept saying 'she shot her'. Blessing's gun was in the car and we have no women on the team. So, I checked the cameras. Imagine my surprise when I watched a ghost kill my mama."

"Sinaya, what are you talking about?" Blessing asked, looking genuinely puzzled.

"Daddy, you didn't-" Sunjai said before I interrupted her.

"No, *they* did; it wasn't just him. *They* led us to believe that Celeste died giving birth to Blessing." Young stormed out the building with Aimee following. "Sunjai, that can't be true since we share the same mother, right? You don't even have to answer that. I watched her kill Annette; I know the bi- Celeste, their mother, ain't dead. As for Blessing and I, we buried our mother with Neema. She may have done a lot of things, but she never abandoned us." Grabbing my purse, I threw the tapes from the day of the shooting on the table and walked out with Ghost right behind me. Blessing could have this shit and she could have that family because I was going home to mine.

Chapter 12

Blessing

"What the fuck!" I screamed, throwing the chair that Sin once occupied across the room.

"Aye, I know you have a lot on your mind, but what I ain't having is you going back to the hospital; calm your ass down." Streetz said, reminding me he was in the room and I was still under the doctor's care.

"Not right now Juelz," I said before heading to the door to catch up with Sin. My heels must have announced my presence because she spun around and looked at me with tears in her eyes.

"I know you're mad; I knew you would be mad as soon as I told that lie in the hospital. Truth be told, if I could do things differently, I wouldn't."

"I deserved to know my mother was still alive Sinaya." I said, fighting back my own tears. I didn't know if I was frustrated or sad but, either way, I refused to cry.

"That's a matter of opinion; if you ask me, you didn't deserve that shit. You didn't deserve for your heart to be played with. You didn't deserve to know the people who were supposed to hold us down, no matter what, and decided not to. Not that they weren't able, we fucking see they were able to be parents; they just didn't want to be ours. And you damn sure didn't deserve to know that his ass came back and was still keeping secrets. Nah, you ain't

89

deserve none of that shit. And, truth be told, the only reason Sincere ain't eating a full clip is because Ghost took my fucking gun. But tell his bitch ass look both ways before crossing the street. And your mother ain't alive; fucked up as the situation was, we buried her with my goddaughter. Clear out the warehouse; we'll go to another one starting tomorrow. I don't like snakes knowing my location," she finished as she walked over, kissed my cheek, and walked back over to the car where Ghost was waiting with the door opened. I really hope they got it together; those two were the hood Michelle and Barack.

"Want me to shoot him in the ass? Nobody goin have my baby mama crying but me, when I'm digging in them guts," Streetz said from behind me, making me laugh despite my situation. I loved that man with every fiber of my being. Coming home from the hospital had been easy, thanks to him. Noah was well taken care of, even when I couldn't jump up for every cry, and he made sure to take me see Neema and Annette whenever I asked.

"Nah, but give me a second to handle this business," I said, walking back into the warehouse.

"This is fucked up; you had us here smiling in their face and left us out of the loop. You know how fake that makes me and Young look?" Sunjai's short frame looked so much taller, as she stood toe to toe with Sincere.

"I understand you're mad, but watch your fucking mouth; you are still my daughter and you, more than anyone, know how I give it up."

"Yeah, you are certainly right. I knew there was a reason you were letting Sinaya get away with so much disrespect. Your ass feels guilty, so you know you deserve that shit."

"Sunjai, he's right. Sincere is still your daddy and he was a good one, at least to two of his kids. Don't disrespect him on the strength of the fucked up shit he and his wife did to us. Fuck, look at us, maybe Annette raising us was for the better because we are some fucking bosses. We don't blame you or Young and would love to build a relationship with you two," I said before facing the man who I was growing to love. "I was happy when your ass appeared out of thin air and, just like the magician you are, here you go again with your tricks. You had tons of time to tell me she was still alive, but you didn't. Make sure when you go back, you tell her we only have two new additions to the family, Sunjai and Young; they will be welcomed with open arms. As for you two, my mom was murdered by your wife and my daddy is as good as dead; I never met the pussy." I finished snatching the tapes off the table and stormed out of the warehouse before he could even say a word. Fuck them, my parents been dead.

"You know you don't have to watch them, right?" Streetz said later that night while I stood in front of the television, hesitant to press play.

"I have so many unanswered questions so, yes, I do have to watch this," I said, finally hitting the play button and taking a seat. I watched the look of shock on Annette's face as she opened the door for the man who I now knew was her father, Emmanuel.

91

Unfortunately, the tapes had no sound, so I was just watching everything play out. I noticed the door opened again a short time later and I walked in, then attempted to sneak up the staircase when they both came around the corner; Emmanuel pointing a gun at me and Annette pointing one at him. Moments later, the door was kicked open by Rock and the team.

"Fucking right!" Streetz's dumb ass clapped like this was a movie. I focused back on the t.v. and saw the reason the bullets first started flying, as a group of Haitians started shooting and Rock and my men started laying them out.

"Awe shit," Ghost said as my mouth fell open. Annette lifted her gun to take a shot at Emmanuel when he ran for the back door, firing behind his back; it was then that two bullets hit me. Annette dropped her gun and attempted to run to my side when a bullet entered her head. My heart dropped as Sincere and Celeste walked through the front door and laid out the remaining Haitians. I stopped the tape after watching Rock break down over Annette's body until his eyes landed on mine. I could tell he was in disbelief because he kept shaking his head, as tears rolled down his face.

I sat there staring at the blank screen for what felt like hours before Streetz walked back in the room, lifted me up, and carried me to the bathtub. I didn't even notice he had slipped away, but the water was already waiting with rose petals inside of it and candles surrounding the tub. The soft music he had playing really put me in my feelings. We had come so far since the shooting and his efforts weren't ignored. I looked around as he stripped me from my clothes and placed me in the warm water. Despite how I was feeling, I had to laugh because this nigga had a 40 sitting in a bucket full of ice. Except, it wasn't an ice bucket, this nigga filled the damn mop bucket with ice. No matter how much money Streetz had, he would forever be hood.

"Ma, what the hell you laughing at? I went all out for you," he smirked.

"Juelz, the mop bucket though son," I said as we both burst out laughing. "And then you have a whole 40 in here; this ain't Boyz in the Hood."

"Shit, you ain't gotta worry about that because that ain't for you; I got you rose petals, music, and these funky ass candles. Keep yo cocked eyes off my damn drink. The mop bucket liquor ain't even yours so don't judge it," he said, stripping out of his clothes and getting behind me in the garden bathtub.

"No but, for real, thank you, baby; I really needed this," I said, turning slightly to place a kiss on his thick lips. Juelz knew he was too sexy for words and I couldn't wait until the doctor released me. It had been too long since I fucked my man and, with the built up pressure I had, Juelz was going to be on bed rest when I finish with him.

"Aye, stop looking at me like that; you know you're on punishment with yo halfway handicapped ass. You just started walking right and, if I put my mans in your life, right back to a wheelchair your ass go." He ducked a punch I threw his way. "Aye, chill with that shit before I drown your ass. Nah but, for real, how you feeling about all this shit?"

"I don't know how to feel. I'm used to not feeling shit. I get mad; I catch a body. I get happy; I catch a body. It rains outside; I catch a body. My first reaction was to kill them; I really wanted to kill my parents."

"Aye, you remember that you're a female right?" Streetz asked me, taking his drink to the head.

"And what the fuck is that supposed to mean?" I asked laughing.

"Shit, that means ya'll all sensitive and shit. It's okay to want to meet and get to know your mother. You have a second chance that people don't get to have; I think you should meet with them."

"I'll call Sin and see what she says about this. I doubt if she'll go with it, but I do want to meet them."

"Since that's situated, how long can you hold your breath?" he asked, stroking his dick and causing my mouth to immediately water.

Chapter 13

Sincere

I already knew I was public enemy number one but, anything I did, I did for my family. There was so much more to the story than Sinaya knew or I wanted her to know. I'd definitely been watching the way Sinaya and Blessing had been making moves and couldn't have been more proud of them. With watching them, I knew that Sin had my ruthlessness and her mom's stubbornness, so getting her to listen to logic wouldn't come easily. Sure, we could have fought tooth and nail for them but, with Emmanuel's army and the feds closing in on us, I had to make sure we didn't end up locked up or dead. Yeah, it's true Celeste was alive and doing better than ever, but that wasn't always the case. When we first left town, Celeste was in a coma from the amount of drugs that Annette gave her, and I couldn't stay around and allow her to finish what she attempted to do. My wife was and always would be my partner in crime so, if Annette was to succeed, they would have to dig two graves. Under no circumstances was I risking my wife dying. I never meant to hurt any of my kids but, as dysfunctional as it was, I was the head of this family and that disrespect shit wasn't about to fly for much longer. I had played grim reaper to too many niggas for less.

"Young and Sunjai are on their way over," Celeste stated as soon as I walked in the door of the estate we lived on. As soon as we decided to return home, I had our home built from the blueprint Celeste created, complete with a panic room that you could access from just about every room in the house. The front yard housed a security home with at least three armed guards at a time who stayed alert around the clock. Some said what we were doing was overkill but, like I said, I wasn't willing to risk my wife's life.

"Shit went left Lest," I chuckled. "That damn Sinaya could be worse than you and I together. From the night of the shooting, she knew you were alive." I was shocked to see Celeste laughing.

"That's my girl; they don't miss a beat. So, when will we all be having this sit down?" she calmly asked.

"Your daughter damn near screamed at her sister; I would have died had Ghost not took her gun. Let's see how that goes for you though," I said, taking the pre-rolled blunt she was holding out towards me. I didn't care how old I got; this was a habit I didn't care to quit. I could have one foot in the casket and I was still going be looking for my daily session.

"I already told you, you're letting her get away with too much shit because you feel guilty about some things we couldn't control," she said, walking towards the kitchen with me following.

"I don't feel guilty about shit. If I did something, I did it for the sake of my family; we know Annette wanted the girls more than anything and they were safe with her. The thing is, I understand their anger. Shit, let's not act like my mother didn't decide that being a parent wasn't a part of her life plan."

"And the difference is we didn't have a choice; it was to save them. Even if the feds would have gotten us instead of the Haitians, they would have separated them. There really is no telling where they would end up. Shit, now that our big secret is out, they will have no choice but to have this sit down. The right way!" she said, stirring a pot on the stove.

"What you over there cooking? Yo ass told me this morning you wasn't cooking shit, but these big ass children say they are coming over and you pulling out the good pots," I joked. I guess losing the girls made her that much more of a protective mother. When they were first born, Sunjai and Sincere Jr. didn't have a chance to complete a cry before she was all in their face. They grew up wanting nothing and, even now in their adult years, they were babied.

"You jealous or something daddy?" she asked, smirking at me. "Sunjai asked for her favorite, crawfish etouffee, potato salad, and fried fish," she said, making my stomach growl. For a few years, we had lived in Lafayette, Louisiana and had put a team together down there. While I was out working, Celeste found a cookbook and learned all the cuisine. She never let me forget how much she hated being home either, but I needed her at 100 percent before she could be by my side again.

"It smells good in here!" Sunjai called, as she walked in to the kitchen and kissed her mother. "Hey ma, how are you today?"

"I'm good baby; the food will be done soon. We can eat as soon as Junior gets here."

"Good because a nigga starving," Young said, walking in and kissing Celeste with Aimee following.

"Sincere, what the hell happened to you and Aimee?" she asked, noticing the bruise under Young's eyes and Aimee's swollen cheek. "I know you two weren't putting your hands on each other. No, fuck that; Sincere, I know you didn't put your hands on a woman!" She moved towards Young as he ran behind Aimee.

"Ma, be cool bruh, you spazzing for nothing. I don't hit Aimee; might choke her ass out for a second, but that's it. Your child needs fucking anger management," he said.

"Yeah, it was your oldest daughter who did this. She better hope I never catch her on the streets, because-" Aimee started

"Because you ain't goin do shit. Ma, you should have seen Sin. I think she's worse than you; she beat Aimee and Young's ass!" Sunjai said laughing. Seeing the puzzled look on her mom's face, she continued. "When we went to the hospital, Aimee called Sin a bitch because she was hating. When we went to lunch earlier, Young's nasty ass was damn near drooling over his sister, so Aimee was intimidated. Anyway, Sin told her when she didn't have her kids, she would beat Aimee's ass. Well, she didn't have her kids today." Sunjai laughed. "And Young wanted to play super save a hoe and stop her from hitting Aimee, so he got a lick too."

"Sunjai, yo ass was supposed to lay her ass out for putting hands on me. What kind of sister are you?" Young laughed.

"Shit, she your sister too. Plus, you see how she was throwing those licks? You lucky you dodged the first one because she wanted to take your head off your shoulders. I told you a long time ago to teach Aimee how to fight too. How you let a grown woman slap you?"

"Leave Aimee alone; I have a feeling if she would have swung on Sin, Blessing would have shot her ass anyway," I finally spoke up.

"Oh, now you know your kids," I heard Sunjai mutter.

"What was that? I didn't hear you."

Chapter 14

Ghost

"Welcome to Chili's, would you like a seat at the bar while you wait on your party?" the hostess asked, all smiles. It took everything in me not to laugh in her face; baby girl was midnight black with bleach blonde hair and green contacts. She looked like a fucking Xbox standing there all smiles.

"Nah shorty, I came to pick up an order under Peaches." I slide her my card just as my phone beeped, letting me know I had an incoming text.

Wifey: Hey baby what are you up to?

Me: Ain't shit, getting me some food. Wyd?

Wife: Still waiting in this slow ass Dr.'s office for my yearly. What are you eating?

Me: Your ass don't care you just bored lol.

Wife: Lmfao. Well screw you too. Be careful, love you.

Me: Love you too, now get that pussy in check lol.

Shit at home for the past few months had been real good, with the exception of that nanny Sin wouldn't fire; I really hated that old hoe. The girls loved her so much; when I suggested we let her go, all three of their asses wanted to kill me. Even Noah loved her old ass. Even though we were moving forward, I knew Sin was hiding something. If Sinaya ain't nothing else, her ass was as vindictive as they came; so, for her to just disappear for two weeks, then come home with no arguments or anything, I knew someone held her attention. I knew I did my dirt, but Sinaya one better stay buried, for the sake of all parties involved. My phone beeped again.

Juelz: Hey bring me some ranch to go with my Southwest Eggrolls plz.

The fact that I had to change Peaches' name in my phone let me know I was still fucking up in my own way. I shook my head, knowing if I told Sin's ass I was getting me and Peaches food, that would be the last words I ever spoke. I wasn't messing with Peaches like that anymore, but I was looking out for her. When Red's crazy ass shot her, she killed our baby and ended Peaches' chances at any other kids she thought she may have wanted. I knew that some of the blame had to be put on me for that shit. Yeah, Peaches was a grown ass consenting adult but, at the end of the day, I knew my girl wasn't playing with a full deck and I dragged Peaches back in the middle of the drama. I couldn't say that I was sad she was no longer having my baby, but I wasn't heartless; a nigga felt guilty as fuck. My guilt drove me to be in this fucked up situation I was in. When Sin came back home two months ago, I heard her put money on Peaches' head, so I stashed her at my house since I wasn't using the shit. As soon as she was back in good standing, I would throw her some money to skip town. I looked up just as the hostess came back with my bag and my card and headed to Peaches.

"Damn, you made it here quick," Peaches said as I walked into the guest bedroom she was occupying.

"Yeah, I need to be back home before Red leaves the doctor and kills my ass," I chuckled, pulling out her food.

"I'm eating alone?" she asked as I was heading for the door.

"Ma, this ain't no date shit. I told you I have to beat Red home."

"Well, I just thought you should know I'm feeling much better and I should be fine to leave tomorrow." She shocked me; I thought I would have to threaten her to leave.

"Yeah? You already decided where you're going?" I walked back to the room and sat on the edge of the bed.

"I'll most likely move to Texas near my cousin. I have nothing left here, unless you changed your mind." She laughed but it didn't touch her eyes, so I know it wasn't all a joke.

"Nah, you should definitely move with your family; I'll run you some bands since I'm damn near to blame for you having to relocate," I said.

"Well, look at you. I remember a while back a nigga refused to pay for my funky ass refill and here you are throwing bands. You must really feel bad." She laughed as my phone rung to Case's *Happily Ever After*. I swear, Sinaya was so hard in the streets, but she made that soft ass song her ringtone in my phone. I looked as Peaches as she did the zipping motion across her lips, then answered my phone.

"Wassup Red?" I asked.

"We need to talk like yesterday; where are you? I'll come meet you," she said in one breath.

"I came to my crib to grab some shit out the safe; don't drive way out here, I'll meet you at home in a second," I quickly said. I wasn't ready to plan my own funeral anytime soon.

"Well, my doctor's office is closer to your place than mine anyway-," she started before I cut her off.

"Red, just do what I said, meet me home." I was greeted by the beeping of my phone, letting me know Sinaya had hung up on me.

"Trouble in paradise; you know what happened last time ya'll had issues, right?" Peaches asked with a grin.

"You'll never know and there won't be a repeat of that episode ma. Let me get out of here…" I started until I heard what sounded like a motorcycle. I quickly looked out of the window and my heart damn near beat out of my chest as I saw Sin checking her gun next to the brand new pink and black Suzuki ninja she just copped herself. "Man fuck, stay quiet," I said, running down the stairs and towards the front door to stop Sin from coming in.

"Oh, hey baby, I was just heading out." I acted surprised to see her, as I blocked her entry into the house.

"You were? Well, since I'm here, let's stay a while. I really need to talk to you," she said, trying to look behind me, but I led the way out the door and shut it behind me.

"Nah, I'm tired and want to see my girls; we can talk at home. Let's go; I'll follow you," I said, watching her get on her bike and rev it up as I got in my truck to follow; I'll just come back for my shit later. I couldn't even lie; I was happy as fuck Peaches decided to leave sooner rather than later, so my home life could go back to normal. Running around hiding shit from Sinaya's CSI ass was more stressful then moving bricks and watching for the feds. I was pulled out my thoughts when Sinaya busted an illegal u-turn in the street. I was about to call her until shit clicked in my head and I knew I was fucked; Sin ain't buy shit I was selling and she was headed towards the house. Hitting a u-turn, I knew I wasn't going to catch her. I watched as she weaved in between cars and avoided lights, while I was playing catch up in a damn Tahoe. Jumping out of my truck, I made it back at my house just in time to hear about 6 gunshots and was met with a locked front door and my spare key gone.

"Man fuck!" I screamed, just as Sin emerged from the house and turned towards me, holding the same gun I assume she just killed Peaches with. I knew my girl; this wasn't a social visit. Peaches got away once; there would never be a second chance.

"Move out of my way Deion." She motioned for me to walk towards the garage with the gun." "I wanted to tell your ass I was pregnant, but I was nervous," she said, taking me by surprise and, despite the fucked up situation we were in, a nigga was happy as hell.

"Baby, I swear we weren't fucking. I felt guilty about what happened to our baby, so I was helping her until she left town," I quickly explained but knew I fucked up when her eyes went black and she started pacing.

I am more than my anger

I am more than my anger

I am more than my anger

I am more than my anger

"I thought that wasn't your child?" she asked, letting me know I fucked up. What I wasn't expecting was the laughter that followed. "Not to worry, the bitch is in there looking like face off. If they find no face, then they have no case, right? I was nervous to tell you I was pregnant because I fucked up but, shit, we both did so what the fuck? We are more than even now. Ghost, don't bring your ass to my house; I'll call you when it's time to do a DNA test."

"What the fuck you mean a DNA test Sinaya?" I screamed, causing her to lift the gun and point it at me again.

"It means congrats; you're one of two men who might be my baby's father." I stood there in shock for a moment, trying to process what she said before I flipped the fuck out. Running towards her, she shot a warning shot so close, it grazed my right ear.

"You know my aim is as official as the navy seals daddy; test me if you want and you can go meet your baby mama," she said, backing up towards her bike with the gun still trained on me. "Back that ass up and get on your knees by the garage, so I can go check on my daughters."

"You goin have to sho-" I started until another bullet grazed my left ear, causing me to get on my knees by the garage. I wasn't scared of any nigga or bitch, but the look in Sin's eyes let me know her ass snapped a while ago.

"Shit, it ain't goin worry me to catch another body. I'll raise all three of my kids." I watched her grab my keys out of my truck, then she hopped on her bike and peeled out of my yard. Watching her turn the corner, everything hit me like a ton of bricks. I couldn't even be happy that Sin was pregnant because the kid probably wasn't mine and what hurt more than anything was that it was my fault.

Chapter 15

Streetz

"I feel like what would help you get better faster in some vitamin D."

"You always trying to be mannish; go brush your grill first nigga." Blessing laughed while covering her nose.

"Yeah alright, don't sit there and try to act like that mouth not hot over there. Shit, I was just trying to be nice, but you damn near made my eyes water with that shit," I said, popping her with a pillow from the bed.

"You talked to Ghost lately? I think those two must have gotten into it again. Last time I talked to Sin, she didn't sound like herself. I asked her what was wrong, but it seems like ya'll all on operation don't stress Blessing out," she said pouting.

"I'm trying to get my dick wet and your ass wanna talk about other people relationship issues," I joked before I heard the doorbell ringing, followed by banging on my front door. Climbing out of bed with Blessing, I ran to the door before the banging woke up Noah's lil blocking ass. Anytime Blessing thought of giving me some ass, here his lil crybaby ass would go. Nigga would start crying and I would never see a tear fall, but Blessing was always falling for the shit. Swinging the door open, I was shocked to see Ghost; he never just stopped by without calling.

"What the fuck is wrong with you?" I asked, looking him over. He looked worse than he did when Sin left him for getting Peaches pregnant. I could tell he was higher than giraffe pussy by how low his eyes were and the fact that I caught a contact just from him passing in front of me. And if I didn't catch that smell, I damn sure caught the smell of liquor. Sin was turning my boy into a damn alcoholic.

"Shit is all fucked up Streetz; a nigga don't know what to do anymore. I feel naked out here without Sin. Then, she took my damn kids again," he said while crying. I ain't never seen a man look so broken and damn sure didn't know what to do with his big ass real life crying. You would think she died or something.

"Fuck is you talking about? I thought ya'll squashed that shit and ya'll were cool now?" I asked.

"We are, well, we were good on that Peaches shit, that time. Streetz, I swear I wasn't cheating on Sin no more. Fuck, on the real, she the only one that my dick even get hard for now. But you know I'm a real ass nigga, so I couldn't leave Peaches out there down bad and what happened to her was really on me. She wasn't supposed to get caught up in me and Sinaya bullshit. So, what kind of nigga would I be if I put her in the middle of that shit, then say fuck her after my girl killed our seed?" he rambled on.

"Wait, you gotta make this shit make sense. You sitting here talking in circles and shit. You was fucking with Peaches again?" I hoped this nigga wasn't that dumb. Fuck, if he was cheating, then I

108

didn't know what all the crying was for. You couldn't have a bitch that run the city and think you could keep shit secret for too long.

"Man, fuck no; Sin caught her in my crib, but we wasn't fucking. I hadn't fucked Peaches since the day she told me she was pregnant. But after Sin shot her, I couldn't leave her in the hospital because Sin crazy ass was liable to wake up in the middle of the night, just to go kill her. Like I said, I couldn't have that on my conscious cause that shit was on me. So, after her surgery, I had them move her to my crib, since I was never there, until she got on her feet."

"Nigga, that has got to be the dumbest thing you have ever said and done. Peaches ass knew you were in a relationship so all of this 'you brought her in that drama' shit is dead. She didn't care about what the fuck Sin would do and that's why she kept fucking with you. Her ass wouldn't have gotten shot in the first place, if she wasn't trying to be messy. She must have rolled up on Sin on a good day for her to only shoot her once and walk away."

"Man, I'm not even fucked up over that shit. Before she dipped on a nigga, Sin told me she was pregnant," he said before I saw what I thought was a tear fall from his eyes.

"Nigga, so what you fucked up about that for? She already raising yours, so what's the problem with having another one with her?" I was confused because I knew for a fact Ghost loved Sin and had even spoke about marrying her on several occasions.

"After she took care of Peaches in my fucking house, she basically told me that the baby she carrying may not even be mine. Nigga, I knew she was out plotting her revenge on me; she let that shit go too easy."

"Damn. I know that shit has you bugging but, at the end of the day, nigga, you did this to yourself. You had a good woman and you turned her into this. I heard her crying to Blessing one day about what you did. Nigga, you broke her when you cheated. So, what you about to do now; let her run off with the next nigga? You need to take your ass and sober up, then go find your woman. As a matter of fact, run me them keys and take your ass a nap," I said, snatching his keys. "Take your ass to a guest room and be quiet too cause if you wake up Noah, your ass will be feeding and rocking him back to sleep, I'm going back to bed." I got up shaking my head; Ghost was my nigga, but for him to sit here playing the victim role was weak as fuck. This was his fuck up. Sin ain't never been a snake, so for her to step out w

Chapter 16

Rello

"Fuck, swallow that dick; damn, you nasty," I said as Sasha, this lil freak I was messing with, spit on my dick then sucked it back up. I had been kicking it with her for about a year now and needed something to keep my mind off Sin, so I called her over from some sloppy toppy. This bitch had my toes curling and, just as I was about to bust, I looked up into Sin's eyes. I thought she would be mad, but she smirked and shook her head before turning to leave.

"Aye, watch out." I jumped up, pushing Sasha's head to the side and pulling my dick from her mouth. The look on her face looked like she was the one on the verge of nutting, but I couldn't worry about that at the moment. Sasha was that kind of freak; she told me the taste of my nut made her nut. That's why her ass stayed around. Running to the front door, I swung it open ass naked and I saw Sin's new motorcycle was still sitting up front.

"You could have finished handling your business Rello," Sin's voice came from the kitchen, making me head that way. "And you damn sure could have put some clothes on nigga," she said laughing while making a big ass sandwich in the kitchen.

"Ain't like you didn't see it all before, what's good though?" I asked.

"From the way you were moaning, that bitch sucking your dick was good." She laughed.

"Why are you here Sinaya?" I asked. Not that I had a problem with her being here, but Sinaya hadn't come back here since we came back from that week we left. I knew her and Ghost were together, and I respected that.

"Yeah, why are you here? Actually, who are you?" I heard Sasha ask with attitude from behind me. I counted in my head to five, knowing Sin was about to clown but it didn't come. She just sat on my island Indian style and ate her sandwich in silence. "What the fuck is she, deaf?"

"Sasha, go back in the room; I'll be there shortly," I told her before she said some shit she and I would regret. I remember one time being in the strip club with my niggas and, naturally, there were strippers in our section. Sasha came through with some birds that saw a stripper sitting on my lap, and her ass decided to show out and threw a drink in the girl's face. Luscious jumped up and hit Sasha with a mean left hook. Shit happened so fast; if Sasha wasn't still on her ass minutes later, I wouldn't believe that it had happened. I stopped talking to Sasha for a few weeks, since she wanted to stake claim on some shit she didn't own. The black eye she was rocking for that month should have shut her ass up but, obviously, she figured she would try it with Sin. Difference between Sin and Luscious was with Sin, you never knew if you would get knocked out or if you were taking a permanent nap.

"What you mean go back in the room? Nigga, how the fuck you just leave me in there like we wasn't in the middle of some shit?

Nah, fuck that; your company has to fucking leave. Her rude ass should have called before she stopped by anyway."

"Man, get the fuck-"

"Nah, I got it Rello," Sin said, wiping her hands then jumping down from the island. "Sasha is it? Didn't they ask you to give us a moment alone nicely? If there is one thing I can't stand, it's bitches like you who don't know when to shut the fuck up. Yo mama ain't taught you to stop while you were ahead? Baby, I don't know what you were looking for when you walked your knock kneed ass in this kitchen, but I guarantee you that this ain't that. Better listen to Rello and carry your ass in that room. I will be done with him shortly and he can use your mouth as a fucking daycare then," she finished before running full speed out the kitchen. I went to follow until Sasha stopped me by grabbing my arm.

"Rello, I think you need to put on some clothes before running to see what the bitch wants," she spat loudly for Sin to hear. I shook my head and laughed.

"Ma, you better be gone before she comes back; that's my warning to you," I said before following Sin. Following the noise I heard, I found Sin with her head in a toilet bowl in my master suite.

"Fuck you and that bitch, Rello; I'll get myself together and you never have to worry about me again," Sasha said, passing up the bathroom with her clothes and purse in her hand.

"I'm fucking her up when I get up from here; I heard that hoe call me a bitch," Sin said before she got sick again.

"Shit, it doesn't look like you're ever getting your ass up; let me go get you some water." Heading to the kitchen, I heard the shower running in one of my guest bathrooms and shook my head. "Who the fuck curses you out, then uses your shower? I got something for Sasha ass though," I said to myself, grabbing two cold bottles of water; one for Sin and the other to pour over that damn shower curtain. Walking back to the back, I looked up to see Sin heading my way, or so I thought. Before I could reach her, she had opened the door to the bathroom that Sasha was in. Before I could say anything, Sin cocked back and punched the curtain with a deadly right hook. The shower curtain and rod hit the floor of the shower with Sasha's foot hanging out from underneath it.

"Sorry Rello, but you know I don't do that bitch word. What's wrong with these yamps not having manners?"

"What the fuck is a yamp?" I asked confused.

"Young Tramp," she answered, walking out the bathroom. "Get rid of your company Rello; we need to talk," she said, heading towards my bedroom. Moving the shower curtain, I was able to see Sasha's face and shook my head. How the fuck Sin hit her dead in the eye through a curtain had me crying laughing. It took me a while but, after getting cursed out, Sasha got up and left.

"Alright, what you wanna talk about?" I asked, turning the corner to see her already under the covers asleep. Figuring the conversation could wait, I took a shower then hopped in the bed with her.

114

***

"About time yo ass showed up," Murda clowned as I walked into the warehouse.

"Shit, I had a long morning," I said with a big ass smile. Sin's ass had pissed me off and left before I could even wake up this morning. I was really pissed off because she came interrupt my situation with Sasha, just to fall her ass to sleep then shoot out on me. Sasha called me this morning apologizing, so I let her come through to get me together.

"I ain't mad at ya. A nigga can't have no long mornings at home," he said, shaking his head.

"Nigga, cause you too busy having long mornings elsewhere," Gutta said, walking in. From the moment I had joined Sin's team, these two had been some thorough ass niggas. I tried to make Sin send them to be on my team, but she wasn't letting these two go. She told me they weren't workers, they were her brothers, and all I could do is respect it.

"I told your ass to stop listening to Vanessa pregnant ass; she all sensitive and shit. I came home from the strip club with glitter on me and she been tripping on me since."

"Damn, yeah, over some glitter? Man, all strippers have glittery shit on those damn costumes; she tripping. Remind me to never get a female pregnant son," I said to Gutta while laughing. I'm glad I didn't have to worry about baby mama drama because God knew I would never be equipped for that.

115

"Nah, ask this clown where she found the glitter at," Gutta said, causing Murda to start laughing.

"Nigga, that's way beside the damn point; she be tripping and you know it. And go find you some business; you sitting here airing all my business like you and my bitch shopping buddies and shit. Mind your business nigga, you too Rello." Looking at Gutta, we both burst out laughing.

"Now I know your ass was cheating; where they found the glitter at nigga?" I asked, still laughing.

"Man, I walked in and she wanted to do that Baby Boy shit and smell my dick like her name Yvette. Big ass belly goin drop to her knees, talking about pull out my lil dick. She knows I'm sensitive about that shit. I'm a grower, not a shower. She should have mind her business because she saw a few specks of glitter on my dick and started crying. Who told her to try that t.v. shit? I told Sin to tell her it's too damn late to want to be sensitive about shit, but her funky ass just goin laugh," he said with a serious face.

"You fucking right; I ain't helping yo dog ass, shouldn't have been cheating on my girl. Tell her call me and I'll school her in how to get revenge on that ass," Sin said as she walked in, causing me to shake my head. I'm positive Murda didn't need his wife getting Sin like ideas. I couldn't even focus on what was going on with their conversation cause Sin had on these short ass True Religion shorts that had her ass sitting right, and I noticed her hips had spread a little. I nodded my head of approval at her cause, as usual, Sin was fresh without trying; she was rocking a pair of Yeezy Boosts and a

116

True Religion v-neck, so I could tell she was relaxing today. Sin was all about her clothing, so she would never go anywhere important dressed so casual. The only ice she had on was her Movado watch. For a moment, I forgot she pissed me off last night or that she had a nigga cause I was thinking of all the places we could fuck in the back of the warehouse.

"Yo ass just like playing with fire huh?" Gutta asked, nudging me.

"Fuck is you talking about; you stay talking in riddles. Speak on that shit," I joked.

"You was drooling like a teething toddler; you goin make Ghost fuck you up. Let that shit go because Sin ain't straying from Ghost." As soon as he said that, I felt myself involuntarily smirking. "Stop fucking lying!" he said laughing.

"Nigga, I ain't said shit," I said as Ghost walked in, looking drunk with clothes that had obviously been slept in. I watched Sin shake her head, then head for the seat she normally sat at towards the head of the table.

"Sinaya, why the fuck you ain't been answering my calls?"

"I'm positive you don't want to do this here," she said as Beretta walked in with a nigga I knew from the streets as Young and two females.

"What's going on?" Beretta asked, looking at Sin.

"Nothing; once everyone gets here, we will get started," Sin said while ignoring Ghost, who was still waiting for an answer. The

117

shit was comical to me. Niggas fucked up and couldn't deal with their consequences; granted, I thought they fixed their issues but obviously not.

"Ain't shit getting started until you answer my fucking question Red! Where the fuck you been cause it ain't been home? You been laid up with that nigga? And I know you didn't have my fucking children over there with that nigga!" he said, walking closer in her space. I saw Murda and Gutta stand from the corner of my eye. They minded their business, as long as no one attempted to touch Sin or Beretta. This one wasn't their fight though; Ghost might not know much about Rello, but I could guarantee his ass had heard about my reputation. Niggas think that because they're the boss, they can't get touched, and that may have held some truth if he was my boss. I was self-made and I ain't ever answered to another nigga. We are more like colleagues, so he could either catch this fade or these bullets, either or, but, behind Sin, he will get fucked up.

"My whereabouts aren't your concern, but the girls are at Disneyland with Ms. Lee Ann and, if you'd like, I can give her a call to drop them off to you," she answered with a smile.

"You let them leave the fucking state with her? I told you I didn't like that bitch. And why the fuck can't you watch them, so you can go be a hoe?" he spat. I watched her eyes turn black and quickly made my way across the room to her. Obviously, I wasn't fast enough because she threw a right hook, hitting him in the jaw, and Ghost quickly yoked her up against the wall.

"Ghost, you know how I give it up; let my fucking sister go," Beretta said, as she and the people she walked in with pulled out guns and pointed them towards Ghost. Ghost had to be in a world of his own because he could give a fuck about either gun being pointed at him.

"You fucked another nigga and that could be my seed you carrying Red?" he asked before I hit him with a quick two piece, immediately causing him to drop her. "Pussy nigga, what the fuck I told you about worrying about my bitch?" He turned, throwing up his sets.

"Oh, you got the game fucked up. I ain't worrying about Sin on this one son; I was protecting my seed," I smirked at him.

Chapter 17

Sinaya

"What the fuck Rello, are you stupid?" I spat, attempting to catch my breath. I couldn't believe this nigga aired my business like that. Ghost had fire dancing in his eyes and I was just waiting on him to sprout horns because that nigga looked like the devil himself.

"You were fucking the help Sin?" Ghost asked with a deadly smirk on his face that didn't touch his eyes. I watched as his hands shook uncontrollably and eased my hand into my handbag for my gun. I knew I was in the wrong for putting my hands on him once again, but I'd be damned if I waited for him to react. Yeah, I had some killers in here that would certainly ride for me, but I wasn't in the business of putting my life in the hands of anyone else.

"Oh nah, you want to shoot me. I mean, fuck, there still is a possibility I'm your baby daddy huh?" he said, walking towards me. He must have forgot all about Rello almost putting him on his ass.

"My nigga, I don't know what breed of nigga you take me for, but you ain't putting hands on my baby mama. And you damn sure ain't about to do it like I'm not standing here," Rello said with the biggest fucking smile on his face. I'm talking one of those Tony the Tiger, your great smiles. "Aye that has a ring to it, don't it?" he asked, looking my way.

"Nigga, are you fucking serious right now?" I asked right before Ghost switched directions, heading towards Rello.

"Say Ghost, I'm telling yo ass right here right now; you put your hands on me and I'm going to beat that ass. Then, you won't be allowed around my seed." This nigga was still cracking jokes before Ghost swung a quick right hook, causing him to stumble. Spitting blood out on the floor, I watched as Rello took off his shirt and turned around, only to be met by Streetz gun.

"How you jump your ass in a one on one fight nigga? I was about to put money on Rello; Ghost swung with all his might and couldn't put him to sleep," Young said with a handful of money. This nigga was really about to bet. "Ghost, I know you pissed off with her and shit, but maybe you should take fighting lessons from Sin. I think she hits harder than you. That ain't a good look, my nigga."

"Young, shut your ass up, everything ain't a joke," Aimee said, causing me to really notice that she had a gun in her hand and she looked comfortable holding it, so she damn sure wasn't new to this.

"Rello, please, just chill; I can handle this on my own. "

"Nah I know you can ma but, on the real, you wasn't goin tell a nigga you pregnant with his shorty?" I realized all eyes were on me and started getting pissed off. This was my family in here, but I damn sure didn't need or want everyone in my business.

"Sin, don't get quiet though; this the nigga you was fucking? A nigga I been feeding-" Ghost started turning back towards me but was interrupted.

"Nah, my nigga, you got shit fucked up; ain't a nigga alive that could take the wrap for feeding me. I been getting it out the mud since a youngin and you got me fucked up if you feel like joining ya'll changed some shit. And I see you getting swole at the chest over there, but Streetz ain't what saved you, my baby mama did," Rello said, blowing a kiss my way. That nigga was a whole clown and didn't care that Ghost wanted his head.

"Oh, that shit funny Sinaya? Yeah, you got pissed off that a nigga called you a hoe, but what you call a woman who gets pregnant and can't tell you who her child's father is? Don't worry, you ain't gotta think on it. Cause where I grew up at, we call them some hoes."

"Ghost, you ain't about to sit here and disrespect my fucking sister like that," Blessing said, stepping forward.

"Nah sis, fuck that pussy; nigga mad cause I dipped on him. It's good; he mad I ain't cheat with no weak nigga like the bitch he cheated with. Bitch went out crying her heart out and begging. Nigga, you hurt cause I pulled a you on you; you'll be alright. I had to stomach that hoe carrying your child and bringing that drama to my front door. Fuck, I had to stomach that bitch living in your house after she disrespected me and what I did? Move right on, huh? Let's call an ace an ace and a spade a spade. I'll be that hoe you called me but you pussy. Falling apart at the seams and shit; you ain't a boss Ghost. I walked in here every day after your shit, both times with my head held high! Both times you fucked up, you walked in here looking like shit. Not a nigga or bitch knew what I was dealing with,

122

not even my sister. You know why; cause I'm a fucking boss. I'm made for this shit daddy. You the employee type though, so you wouldn't know shit about that; nigga, you a joke," I spat. My hands were shaking and everything in me wanted Ghost dead on the spot. I watched the hurt in his eyes and immediately wanted to reach out to him, despite my anger, but those feelings were quickly replaced when he said his next words.

"Yo, you boss around a room full of mother fuckers. I'm talking certified killers 24/7 and 365 and, all of a sudden, yo hoe ass wants to play follow the leader? Monkey see, monkey do? I have one child, and you need to call that old bitch and tell her to bring me my child before I have to go looking for her. You ain't got shit to say to me or Breeze until it's time to take the DNA test for that possible you're carrying." I noticed, in his eyes, he regretted the words as soon as they crossed his lips. It was way too late for regret though; he looked me in the eyes and basically said Noelle wasn't his, and the only way he was taking Breeze was over my dead body. Granted, I knew Noelle wasn't biologically his but neither was Breeze, and he had never denied my daughter. Before I could react, the sound of gunfire erupted from outside. I knew they were shooting at the building, but it was pointless; our warehouses were bulletproof because of the bullet resistant fiberglass panels I made sure were installed. Even the windows couldn't be penetrated. Looking out the window, I noticed a group of niggas standing in front of two black Denalis, attempting to light up the building. Turning to Murda and Gutta, I nodded as I grabbed two guns from my bag and made my way toward the back door with them leading, Blessing by my side, and who was here of my team following.

"Sin, where the fuck you going; you're pregnant! You need to sit your ass down somewhere and let us handle this!" Ghost roared.

"Ain't your baby, so don't you fucking worry about it. We both know it ain't nothing to catch a body… or two while knocked up." I laughed, referring to Peaches and her pregnancy I terminated.

"Well, shit, that could be my seed, so I agree with his bitch ass; you need to sit your ass down!" Rello said, staring at Ghost.

"What the fuck; they just dumped a body out, dark skinned man with dreads. I can't make out his face though." Aimee was still looking out the window and had caught all of their attention, as Blessing and I ran for the back door. I didn't need to lay eyes on him to know who that was. These bitches had my fucking brother. Ignoring the screams behind me, I eased the side door open, and Blessing and I snuck around the side of the building, as these niggas made plans to enter the building. The accents they had let me know they were from deep down South and, as I listened a while longer, I heard them mention Snake and Ebony in the same sentence and knew just where their bitch asses had been hiding this whole time, and these men were going to bring me to them. Just as I turned to tell my plan to Blessing, my eyes fell on the lifeless body laid behind them and logic went out the window; they weren't making it out of my parking lot alive. Thank God all the warehouses were in deserted areas because the clean-up crew would have a big job to do.

"Alright, it's about 12 of them; if we aim high, your brother will be good." I turned my head to notice Sunjai, Aimee, Young, Rello, Streetz, and Ghost were behind us. Blessing and I must have been too focused on Rock to hear them approach.

"Sunjai, go back inside and take Aimee with you," I said instead of responding to her idea because I didn't know if my brother was good at the moment anyway.

"Don't sleep on her sis; I can guarantee Sunjai can shoot better than most niggas you know. And just cause Aimee can't fight, don't think she can't handle herself," Young said. I hit his ass with a head nod before Blessing pulled out her twin Berettas and delivered two head shots to both men standing closest to Rock's body. I was shocked as I looked to my left and saw Aimee and Sunjai laying niggas out, right along with us. I didn't even know they had guns, yet along could handle them like they were; Sunjai was over there looking like a baby Blessing. And despite everything, I had to respect Aimee because I didn't even fuck with her, but here she was laying niggas out for us. I couldn't dwell on that because the only thing on my mind was getting to my brother. I didn't know where Ebony and Snake found these dummies, but they should have left them there. We had already knocked five of them off before my team came from the front doors and finished the rest of them off. Running over, I paused when I heard gunshots again and spun around with my gun at the ready, until I noticed Blessing shooting at one of the bodies on the ground.

"Fuck, I thought I saw him move," she said laughing until I saw Rock slightly move from the corner of my eye. Kneeling down next to him, I noticed the track marks on his arm and knew they had been drugging my brother.

"Rock, Rock, wake up for me, my love," I said, shaking him as sweat poured from his face. Hearing my voice, he opened his eyes and they were glossed over.

"Noelle… Breeze…" he mumbled.

"I will get them here as soon as possible. They've missed you too." I smiled through the tears pouring from my face. I was happy he was alive, but there was no telling what else they did to him and that was eating away at me. I should have been looking for him harder than I was. I was supposed to be my brother's keeper and I was fucking up.

"Ebony…" he mumbled again before closing his eyes and shaking uncontrollably.

"Get me a fucking truck and get my brother to a hospital!" I screamed, looking around until I noticed no one else had come over and they were still standing where we left them, huddled together. Leaving Blessing with Rock, I made my way over to see everyone surrounding Aimee, who was the only person on our side to catch a stray bullet. Seeing Young crying his eyes out and everyone surrounding her body had me thinking she was already gone until I heard her coughing

"Fuck is ya'll just standing here like she checked out for? Stop that fucking crying Young! Get Aimee and Rock to a hospital now!" I said to Gutta, who ran around back to get a truck. "The rest of ya'll clean this shit up and burn these niggas. Take the trucks to a chop shop after ya'll run those plates." I ran to the truck as they loaded up Rock and Aimee. Before pulling off, I looked at Ghost. "Your baby mama is dead so if she was your rebound bitch, you can think again, and I hope you're ready to make those funeral arrangements," I said as we pulled off.

Chapter 18

Celeste

Being with Sincere, I learned to deal with a lot of shit a long time ago. My husband was my world and I was his. He was a great provider, partner, lover, and yes, despite the decision we made, a great father also. He did his best to make sure I was prepared in the event of there being a call in the middle of the night saying he wasn't coming home. With that all said, no mother was prepared for the call I just received. Young was very much like his father in many ways, one of those being that he hardly ever showed his emotions. So, when I answered my phone and all he was repeating over and over was that he fucked up and she was going to die before he started loudly crying, my first thought was something was wrong with Sunjai. The bond those two had was stronger than what you would expect from twins. When they were delivered by C-section, they were holding each other. Then, when they got home, they would not sleep if they weren't next to each other. It's like they were each other's safety net because the only way to calm one down was to lay them next to the other. Throughout life, that never changed.

"What's going on?" Sincere asked, hearing me trying to calm Young down. I put him on speaker phone and hopped out of the bed in search of clothes. I tuned them out once I heard Sincere's deep voice telling Young to stop all that crying and speak. He always spoke so harshly to my baby, but I knew he was raising a boss and had to accept that. It didn't take long before my husband joined me in the closet to get dressed.

"Did he tell you exactly what happened?" I finally asked.

"Nah, you know that lil nigga hung up on me for screaming at him," he said, causing me to laugh despite the circumstances. I wasn't exaggerating when I said Young was just like Sincere; he didn't do well with disrespect. Before he would curse out his father for screaming at him, he would disconnect the call.

"I'm worried Sincere. What if it's one of the girls?"

"That thought crossed my mind also. If it is one of them, the city will bleed." He grabbed my hand then turned up the music, letting me know this discussion was over. My husband was a man of very few words and I knew this was tugging at his emotions, so I let it go. What I could guarantee you though was that California did not want to see the old me surface. Sin and Beretta earned their reputation of the boss bitches they were out here but I guarantee, if you heard about them, then you heard whispers about my days in the streets. I knew all about Sin's anger issues and she didn't steal that from anywhere. For the sake of this city, my daughters better be in one piece when I get to them. As worried as I was, the thought of being face to face with Blessing and Sin made a smile form on my face. I didn't even know Sincere was watching me.

"They won't be happy to see you, especially your oldest daughter," he said.

"What the hell you mean my oldest daughter; she's yours too." I laughed.

"Nah, you can have that one; I'm telling you she's the devil in heels. I used to think you were mean. And you saw what she did to Aimee and Young; I almost wanted to tell him to shoot her mean ass." He laughed as we pulled up to the hospital. "No but really, listen, I don't want you to think this will be some big happy reunion because it won't. You may have more of a reaction from Blessing, but Sinaya hides her emotions well. She will ignore you like you never existed. Don't expect much; we will deal with this some other time."

"I understand what you are saying, but I need to make sure they are all okay. Sometimes, I think coming back caused more trouble than it did to solve any problems." I confessed what I had been thinking for a few days now.

"No, there's just so much drama they're dealing with that we would have to wait for it to be resolved in order to have a real sit down. Let's go check on them," he said, coming around to open my door. No matter how many years had passed, I had never touched a door in his presence; I was treated like a queen. Walking in to the hospital, I really didn't know who to ask for at the front desk, so we searched the family rooms until we spotted Young pacing in the hallway.

"Young, what's going on; who has been hurt?" I cried, rushing to his side.

"Aimee, they rushed her to surgery ma. It ain't looking good. I should have listened to Sin and made her ass stay inside. Ma, I clown a lot, but you know what Aimee means to me. That's my rib in there fighting for her life," he said, fighting back tears, and all I could do was hug him.

"Is the family of Aimee Peterson here?" a doctor walked out asking. I felt Young go stiff in my arms and knew he wouldn't answer.

"Yes sir, that's my daughter-in-law; I assume you have an update on her."

"Hello, I am Doctor Robertson and, yes, I do have an update for you; she is out of surgery. She did code twice during the procedure so, for the time being, it is touch and go. Aimee was shot twice; one bullet entered her arm and we successfully removed that one. However, there is another bullet that we have decided not to remove at this time. Removing the bullet may cause paralysis, so we will just closely monitor it to make sure it doesn't migrate. Because of that second bullet, her lungs did collapse, so we have put her in a medically induced coma so that could heal. In a few moments, we will be transferring her to the intensive care unit, where she is allowed one visitor at a time. You will be paged when you can go visit her and, please, let the front desk know to page me if you have any more questions or concerns," he said before exiting through the double doors he had just come out of.

"Young, all she needs is prayer right now; you have to have faith that she will pull through. Besides, you know Aimee isn't just letting some female scoop you up." I tried to lighten the mood and smiled when I saw a genuine smile cross Young's face.

"I should go in her room and flirt with a nurse. I bet her jealous ass would pop up quick, talking about some; 'Is you serious right now, don't get you and her fucked up in here Sincere'." He laughed as he mocked her voice perfectly. Another doctor headed our way while looking down at a clipboard.

"Is the family of Darius Rockwell present?" he asked before I heard multiple chairs scraping and what sounded like people running to the door.

"Yeah, I'm his sister; how is my…" I looked up into the eyes of my daughter, Sinaya, holding hands with Blessing as her voice trailed off. I watched as she fought through her emotions. She went from shock to furious in seconds. "Why the hell are they here?" she spat.

"This isn't the time sis; we are here for Aimee and Rock, remember?" Sunjai said as I looked at Blessing, who was staring at me with tears in her eyes. Sin had an opportunity to know me in her earlier years, but Blessing had never been face to face with me before.

"Blessing, I-" I wanted to say something, explain some type of way, but Sinaya quickly shut that thought down.

"Umm Doctor, how is my brother?" she loudly questioned, interrupting me and pulling Blessing closer to her. I could already tell she was the protector of the two.

"Would you like to step into the room?" he asked, eyeing the large group of men standing behind them.

"No, here is fine; almost everyone here is family," she said, making sure she put emphasis on the almost.

"There were a lot of drugs in your brother's system. We have given him fluid, as he was severely dehydrated, and he is now peacefully sleeping. There is going to be a long road to recovery and I would recommend you signing him up for the rehab here. I'm sure with our facility and a lot of love and support from you all, he can kick this habit."

"Yeah, that's fine; let's sign him up. I'll pay it, no matter the cost," Sincere answered.

"No, he will not. I will be handling all of my brother's expenses sir. Can he have visitors yet?" Sin asked, cutting her eyes at us.

"Yes, as soon as we get him settled in. As this is such a large group, I will have to say immediate family only, at least until tomorrow morning," he said before walking off.

"Let me tell ya'll something; out of respect for Young and Sunjai, you are still breathing. Don't overstep your boundaries and try to be parents of the year. My father ran off on us a long time ago, I just buried my mother, and I'm full fucking grown, so I'm not looking for replacements. Stay in your lane and out of my way," she said, causing me to laugh, and everyone to look at me.

"Sinaya, your angry baby girl; I definitely understand. I would be angry too if I didn't know the whole story and didn't care to listen. But what I won't tolerate is the disrespect. Don't let my height get you fucked up; I'm nothing nice."

"I know all about your past, Celeste, and let me tell you; while impressive, it doesn't make me view you in a different light or anything. You let me know you don't deal with disrespect and that's fine and cool. What am I supposed to do with the information now though? Was that supposed to scare me cause, just like I did my research, I know you've done yours, and Sin ain't been scared of shit since the boogie man. You can keep the threats and the warnings and deliver that speech to someone who has concerns," she said before turning towards two men that were standing behind her. "Murda and Gutta, tell Tech find Lee Ann for me. She know the only rule was to answer when I called and I can't get in touch with her. Rock was asking for the girls and I want them here yesterday," she said, walking off.

"Blessing, can we please talk?" I tried my luck since she was alone.

"Nope, I have to check on the only family I have left," she said, walking away.

"I told you not to expect much. We'll have our sit down, just on a later day. Emotions are running too high," Sincere said, as the first doctor came back out and called us over. Young reached him first and I got there just as my son fell to his knees crying.

"What's going on?" I asked.

"I'm sorry, but Aimee didn't make it."

Chapter 19

Ebony

Me: How far are ya'll?

Smoke: Right down the road from them.

Me: Dump him then go, you have no idea who those people are.

Smoke: Me and Dame decided to take a few down before we hit the road.

Me: That wasn't a part of the plan they are too deep. Drop him then dip.

Smoke: We brought everyone with us, we'll be cool. You said they were the only thing standing in the way of more money.

Me: What do you want your tombstone to say idiot?

Rereading the messages from earlier, I tried again to get in touch with the team that went drop off the package for me, before I heard footsteps coming towards me.

"How was she today?" I asked, standing from the recliner.

"Well, Ebony, she seems to be doing great today; her sugar is regular and she's in a great mood."

"Thank you so much Ashley; see you Thursday," I said, walking my grandmother's home health nurse to the door. I couldn't chance Ghost getting to her after the shit I pulled, so I brought her to stay with me.

"Come on granny, let's go; it's time take a nap," I said, leading her to the room she had been occupying. There really wasn't much in her but a new bedroom set I had bought just for her.

"I don't want to be here Ebony. Take me back to my nursing home; this damn house stinks. And you think I don't know what you all got going on up in here. You're sticking drugs in that boy and he don't want to be here either. What the hell has gotten into you? I pray for you every night, but you just can't seem to get your life together," she spoke, saying more than she's said since being moved here.

"Granny, you must really be tired. I don't know what boy you are talking about. The only guy that's here is Snake."

"Chile, play with yourself; don't play with me. I've bought that boy food and everything when you all leave. And why are you working with that no good boy? When your daddy brought him home, I told him something wasn't right with him. Ebony, I'm worried about you," she finished.

"Granny, I'm fine; take your medicine and go to bed," I said, walking out of the door and closing it behind me. I couldn't believe I was careless enough to let her see Rock here. I was deep in my thoughts and ran right into Snake on my way to the front.

"Didn't I tell you it wasn't a good idea to have her here?" he grilled me.

"And didn't I tell you I couldn't risk Sin, her crazy ass sister, or Ghost getting to my motherfucking grandma!" I snapped back.

This nigga really wanted me to leave my grandmother assed out. Ghost wasn't the type to use families, but I had no idea what those other two bitches were capable of, once they got their package I just sent express mail. I was so tired of Snake and was glad his ass hadn't been here for a week, so I was a lil surprised seeing him here today.

"Well, now she saw him, what if she opens her mouth?"

"Nigga, to who? She literally sits in the house 24/7, so please tell me who she is going to tell. Snake, I keep telling your ass you don't run shit around these parts. Those niggas on your payroll jump when you say jump, I don't. Besides, Rock ain't our problem anymore. I have a better plan," I said smirking.

"What the fuck you mean he ain't our problem no more? What the fuck did you do Ebony? I told you not to make any moves without me being here. You so fucking smart until you dumb," he said, walking to the back to check on Rock. He would be hugely disappointed. "What the fuck did you do? Where the fuck is Rock, you dumb bitch!" Snake spat in my face.

"Shit, he should be dumped off at his sister's front door at this point. While you were out on vacation and shit, I came up with a better plan," I bragged.

"How the fuck is he getting to his sister if your funky ass still here?"

"Smoke took some men and they're dropping him at their warehouse. I don't see the problem; we needed to knock her off her square, so she would be an easy kill and I think this is the perfect way."

"Smoke! That's my best fucking man. You do know they will kill them, right? If killing them were so fucking easy, they would be dead by now. I wouldn't be stuck in fucking bumfuckegypt, and I damn sure wouldn't be stuck with yo deadbeat ass!" he yelled, causing me to smile.

"I gave Smoke one simple ass job and it was his idea to take your whole team on that damn suicide mission. They aren't my concern, as long as they deliver the package, I'm cool." I shrugged because it really didn't make me a difference. I didn't care about none of those niggas; this whole team thing was Snake's idea. He wanted to kill Ghost because he wanted Sin's ass and I simply wanted Sin gone, so I could get my baby daddy back.

"Bitch, I should snap your fucking neck; your job wasn't to come up with ideas. You ain't slick; you let that nigga go because you fell in love. Bitch, I ought to kill your dumb ass. I told Ahmad your plan wouldn't be about shit." What he said wasn't really a lie; I had started to fall for Rock. From the very first moment I stepped to him, I knew exactly who he was. I noticed him in the club with Sin the very first time I saw her, but he was too drunk to notice me. After doing my research and looking him up, I knew exactly who he was and how he could be beneficial to me.

"Snake, I don't see you making moves; you ain't shit but some jealous ass nigga! First you wanted Ghost's throne because you were tired of being his lil bitch boy. If Ghost told your ass to walk on water, your ugly ass would for sure drown trying. So, you stole a lil work and cash from him. Nigga, you bragged on ten thousand shitty ass dollars you stole and ran through already. Do you know how much money he spends on a single mall trip? That nigga has bought me mother's day bags worth more than that and he can't stand me. Do you have any idea how much money that nigga touches? Don't let the hood in him fool you. That nigga was damn near a millionaire when we were together; no telling what those pockets sitting on now. Shit, if you would have asked him for the money, then you would have gotten more than that. So, when they do catch your ass slithering around and kill you, it ain't about the money daddy. It's the principle of it all." I winked at him before walking away.

"Bitch, what the fuck you think will happen to you if I die? You and Ahmad will be dying right alongside of me; guilty by association hoe. You talking all this shit like you ain't on mission get your baby daddy back, like you can just run back to him. But I don't recall him fucking with your stanking ass before Sin came in the picture," he spat.

"When it's all said and done, I ain't goin need to go running to him; he'll come find me." I smirked while hearing a car door slam, announcing that my visitors were back from the store. They had arrived yesterday and this would be Snake's first time seeing them. I had to learn when I was young; never to put all my eggs in one basket.

"Stop talking in riddles and say what you have to say!" he snapped.

"Get the door, you'll be thanking me." After staring at me for a moment, he made his way to the window next to the front door and stared out of it.

"Please tell me that's not what I think it is? Bitch, this is your plan? This the shit you so fucking happy about; you took their fucking children? I'm sitting here worried about Storm and my crew, when they are safer than us. Bitch, even I ain't stupid enough to touch a nigga children. Good fucking job, you about to have that nigga and his retarded ass bitch really come meet us. Then what, you going tell him how much you love and miss him?"

"I just need him to listen to me for one minute and I'm sure I can make him hear me out," I answered, feeling like I fucked up for real this time.

"You really sound stupid as fuck. The only talking that will happen is at your funeral; you seem to forget you didn't just take Ghost's child, you took her child too. Even if he wanted to listen to you, I guarantee you she's not," he said, letting my aunt Lee Ann in with the kids.

Chapter 20

Sunjai

"Who is Ebony and where can I find her?" I asked, pacing. I was seeing red and it wasn't just from Aimee's blood that I saw every time I closed my eyes.

"You remind me of myself pacing like that. Now, I see why it works on Blessing's nerves," Sinaya said calmly, while staring out the window of the hospital suite we were in.

"How are you so calm right now? I get that you hate Aimee, but aren't you mad about what they did to your brother?" It was really bothering me that she was still sitting at the window, smiling and shit at nothing.

"If you see me as being cool, calm, and collective, you can thank Dr. Cruze for that. I guess all those years of therapy were effective. I didn't hate Aimee; she was just going to have to respect my mind before I accepted her. What you see as me being calm, baby girl, is only what I am showing you. Never let them see you down and out because they would love to use that against you. Being a boss means having your poker face on at all times. You have to stay unpredictable, so they can't point out your next move. Right now, Ebony expects me to come after her so she's hiding. Don't worry because I will grant her that wish but, right now, I'm imagining different ways to kill her. I can't really decide just yet." She smiled at the window again.

"And they call me crazy; is that what your loony ass in here giggling and laughing about? Why can't you just shoot her and get it over with?"

"That's not really fun, is it? Besides, that's too damn cliché. I have some ideas, but I'm leaning towards the later," she said.

"Do I even want to know what you are planning on doing?" I asked, laughing at the smile that crossed her lips.

"I thought you would never ask. I was thinking since they drugged my brother, I would tie her ass to the back of a car and drag her for a few blocks. I saw that shit on a movie once and always said I would try it. That shit was tight! But then, I thought she stabbed him with needles, so I could do the same to her," she said.

"So, that's your revenge; you going get her addicted to drugs?"

"Hell no, she might like that shit; I'm killing her ass with a nail gun. I don't know how to use that shit, but I'll YouTube it." She smiled, but I saw her fighting back tears.

"Have you talked to Ghost?"

"Fuck Ghost! I'm going get something to eat from the cafeteria. Do you want anything?" She quickly changed the subject.

"Nah, but this conversation ain't over Sin!" I screamed to her back. Once she was gone and I had my thoughts to myself, it took everything in my power not to break down. Aimee was like a big sister to me and knowing my twin was hurt was really touching my soul. I blamed myself for a moment because she only rushed outside because I told her let's go. I lived for this shit and Aimee was just an around the way chick, trying to be my brother's rider. As I wiped the tears from my eyes, I heard movement from behind me and spun around to see my parents at the door.

"How is he?" I asked while clearing my throat.

"You know your brother; if he's hurting, you'll never know," my mom said, fighting back tears of her own. My parents basically raised Aimee from the age of 14, when her mom and dad decided they didn't want to be parents anymore and just moved out of town while she was in school. Once I got older and found them, I took care of them properly. I know you're wondering how did I do that, but we'd get into that later.

"Nah, I'm positive he's hurting. I can feel that shit in my heart."

"Where is Sinaya? I was wondering if I could talk to her," my mother asked, and I saw the tears in her eyes. I understood why they had to leave, but I also understood where Sin was coming from. My mom and dad had hurt her like Aimee's parents hurt her. At least Aimee knew the truth and got stronger from that. Sin never really dealt with what she thought was the death of her mother. And to find out she went on and had children would have my parents getting buried the very next day.

"Give her some time ma; she'll come around. You can't rush this and you don't have the rights too anyway. She took many years trying to move on from your death and may take that many more to cope with you reappearing," I said, just as I heard coughing from behind the curtain. Walking over, I pulled it back to see Rock fighting with the restraints that were holding him to the bed. When he woke up, he began to attempt to remove the IV's from his arms and, in the process, knocked over machines, so he was sedated again. We were warned that the meds they provided wouldn't last long, as he was going through withdrawals of the drugs they pushed in his system.

"Noelle... Breeze... Baby..." he said as his eyes searched the room.

"Rock, I'm Sunjai, Blessing, and Sin's sister. They are trying to get in contact with Lee Ann so that we can get the girls here," I said, attempting to calm him down.

"No... Ebony has Noelle," he said again before shaking horribly.

I was pushed to the side by my mother, who started looking through his belongings bag until she pulled out a crumpled piece of paper.

"Sunjai, do you know who is this Ebony person is?" she asked, reading over the paper.

"Yeah, that's Ghost baby mama; what's that in your hand?" I asked, walking over.

"A bill for home health services; there's an address, but it's in Louisiana and it's written out to a Lee Ann," she said, handing the paper to my father. "The nanny's name is Lee Ann and, all of a sudden, she isn't answering the phone; I don't believe in coincidences. I bet anything he saw those babies before they kicked him out. Why you think they let him go? He was no use to them because they had bigger bait. But Sin isn't falling in that trap. We are going get my grandbabies." I looked up as my father walked back in the room; I hadn't even noticed he left.

"I have someone watching the house, let's go. Khaoz has a jet here already and she's letting us use it. Don't say anything to Sin until we know for sure," he said, referring to one of the best finessers in the game. I could tell her story, but that deserved a book of its own. Looking back at Rock, I watched as he seemed to have fallen back asleep, before I ran behind my parents.

Hopping on the jet, the only thing on my mind was my sister; I wouldn't let anyone hurt her again. After going over the plan for what felt like the tenth time, I put on my headphones and zoned out. I always got this way before a kill. See, what only my family knew was that I wasn't some teenage daughter of a boss. I was a trained killer. I knew all about Blessing because we ran in the same circle; she would just never be able to place a face to my name. I was known as Shadow to the organization that provided the contracts. Of course, I didn't need the money; I just liked the thrill of the kill. I had to laugh to myself; my family was just all kinds of fucked up. I wasn't really surprised to find out that Streetz was also in the business. Almost every circle of people involved in the drug game had at least one hired gun on their team. My father never had problems with his teams because I would get rid of any threats to my family's success. I must have dozed off because I woke up to my father letting me know it was show time.

"Okay, Sunjai, here is your car. The clothes you need are on the inside. All you have to do is get in and leave the door unlocked. Try to get all the kids in one room without raising any suspicion, ok?" my mother asked, pointing to a 2016 Chevy Malibu.

"Yeah, I got it. You two been out the game for a while; ya'll think ya'll can handle this?" I asked, halfway joking. Although I knew what they were capable of, I always worked alone so this should be fun.

"Where you think you learned it from? You just make sure that all the doors are unlocked. We'll be coming in from the front, side, and back doors," my father said as I made my way to the car. It didn't take me long to change into the nurse's uniform and fresh white pair of Nike's behind the heavy tint of the car, and I was on my way to the destination with help from my GPS. Hopping out, I noticed a car sitting a few houses down and nodded, knowing it was my father's men. Ringing the doorbell, I didn't expect for a man to open the door. The team told us it was just her and the kids. The man sitting in front of me was just as ugly as could be and it took everything in my power not to grimace when he spoke, and I saw the plaque buildup on his crooked teeth.

"Who the fuck are you?" he spat.

"Hey, I'm Jasmine; I thought the office gave you a call and let you all know Ashley was no longer with us. I'll be taking over the care for Ms. Clara and it's routine that I come in and see exactly what I'm dealing with before actually accepting the patient. Where is she located?" I asked, pushing my way in the house since he wasn't going to step aside.

"In the back room to the left," he said from behind me. Looking over my shoulder, I saw his eyes on my ass as he followed. A little girl walking into the room opposite of where he was sending me caught my attention; she was the spitting image of Sinaya. "Umm, I didn't catch your name, unless you want me to just call you handsome," I lied through my teeth ass he smiled, then answered.

"The name is Snake, but you can call me handsome if you'd like. I get that a lot." He knew his ass was lying. Heading down the hallway, I heard the crying of a baby and knew that it was Noah, Blessing's son.

"Well Snake, can you get me a bottle of water?" I asked, hoping that would get me enough time to look for the kids. Instead of answering, he just walked away. I quickly made my way to the door that was slightly ajar and saw all three kids on a dirty mattress. Closing the door back just in time, Snake handed me the bottle of water. "Before you go, I need to wash my hands; where is your restroom?" He rolled his eyes, then pointed back towards the front where we came from. After passing and unlocking the doors I was supposed to, I headed to the restroom. Quickly turning on the water, I texted my father about the additional man, then called Sin.

"We are already on the way; don't kill anyone! I want them all alive," she ordered as soon as she answered the phone.

147

"Done," I said and hung up the phone and put it in my bra, just as the door swung open and my eyes connected with Snake's. "Umm, can I help you?" I asked with attitude.

"Who are you talking to?" he asked, looking towards the window.

"I said I was done after washing my hands. In nursing school, we're taught to say our alphabets to insure our hands are clean and I simply said done when finished," I said, walking out and towards the room he told me housed Ebony's grandmother. Opening the door, I saw she wasn't alone, but what pissed me off was the fact that this man was in the room having sex on the same bed, as who I assumed was Ms. Clara, was sleeping on. Pulling out my gun and my phone, I called in my back up.

Chapter 21

Sinaya

My mind was going in a million and one direction as I plotted out how I was killing everyone involved in the kidnapping of my children and nephew. Blessing had checked out long ago and what remained behind was Beretta, a cold hearted killer. Since we hopped on the jet, she hadn't said a word and I couldn't blame her. She had already lost one child before she met her and here it was, months later, her son was kidnapped. I wanted to still be mad at Sincere and Celeste, but how could I when they had saved my children's lives?

"You know your baby mama isn't getting spared, right? That bitch will beg for me to kill her when I'm done with her," I spoke to Ghost for the very first time since the argument at the warehouse.

"I'm putting the final bullet in that bitch's head," he answered without taking his eyes off of the road. We had arrived in Louisiana and there was already a car waiting for us with the address to an abandoned building programed into the gps.

I am more than my anger

I am more than my anger

I am more than my anger

I am more than my anger

I had been repeating the chant in my head since I walked in Rock's room and found the receipt with Lee Ann's name sitting on the ground. It didn't take a genius to realize why Rock kept saying the girl's name when he first woke up. He had already seen them and Lee Ann and, for that, she was paying with her life. As soon as I heard 'you have reached your destination', I jumped out of the vehicle before Ghost could even park and was running in the building with Blessing following close behind me.

"Where are the kids?" I asked to the room full of people.

"We have them at a hotel room with mom," Sunjai answered, coming from a back room with blood on her clothes. I headed towards the room she was coming from and immediately sent a bullet through Lee Ann's skull. When I saw blood splatter from her chest also, I looked to my left to see Blessing lowering her gun also.

"Damn, that's really your daughters," I heard one of the men behind me say.

"Sunjai, you have that shit I asked you for?"

"Yep," she said, throwing the duffle bag at my feet. I made my way towards the rest of my guests and was beyond excited when my eyes landed on Ahmad.

"Where did you find him?" I asked with a smile.

"He was fucking Ebony here in her grandmother's bed, while she was still laying in it," she said with disgust written all over her face. Looking closely at Ahmad and Ebony's face, I knew that's where the blood came from.

"Bitch, you was laid up there fucking with my kids in the next fucking room?" I asked, punching her in the face so hard, the

150

chair she was tied down to fell backwards. "What if my daughters walked in on that sick shit?"

"He raped me; the sick bastard has been raping me since I was fifteen. I thought when I moved I had finally escaped him, but the sick bastard followed me. He ended up at the same rehab I was in and the rape started again. Anytime he could, he was sneaking in my room. Then, I found out I was pregnant. I wanted to tell you she wasn't yours, but you were so happy and, once she was born, no one could tell you anything about her. I know you hate me for that, but there was so many times I wanted to tell you but I didn't," she pleaded.

"Bitch, you brought them around that nigga and you knew he was a rapist?" Before she could get another word out, Blessing was raining blows on her.

"Ebony, your ass been on borrowed time, but you fucked up by kidnapping Rock, then my children. Breeze has no need for you anymore; she has a mother. Your services are no longer needed," I said, reaching into the bag and grabbing the nail gun. "I figured since you wanted to stick needles in people's body, I would show you how that felt."

"Ghost, don't do let her do this! I am the mother of your child. I love you!" Ebony started pleading her case.

"Nah bitch, I ain't fucking with him right now, but don't bump your dick suckers to my man," I said before shooting her in the feet with the nail gun. "Sunjai, this is easier than I thought! Told you YouTube teaches you everything you need to know," I said over her screams, then laughed before shooting Ebony in the middle of her forehead with the nail gun, instantly killing her. I looked at Ghost to see if there was any remorse in his eyes and there was none.

"Who's next?" Sunjai asked with a smile

"These females really are fucking nuts. Like the whole fucking family needs help," I heard Streetz tell Ghost and started laughing.

Going into the bag Sunjai got for me, I grabbed a butterfly knife and a rusty machete, then made my way to a naked and unconscious Ahmad. He wouldn't be asleep for long though.

"If you are easily disgusted, then I suggest you leave the room like yesterday's time. Because I can guarantee you, it's about to get real nasty." I watched as a few men walked out, but Sincere walked a little closer. "Sincere, meet Ahmad; the biological father to your first grandchild Noelle. Let me tell you how we met. I was enjoying my 22nd birthday in a club where I got drunk and drugged. I knew something was wrong, so I tried to leave. While attempting to get home, I was stumbling to my car when he took these fingers and led me to an abandoned building." I paused for a second as I began cutting off Ahmad's fingers with the butterfly knife. Halfway through the first finger, he began screaming and attempting to move his hand away. After ignoring his screams and making it through all five fingers, he blacked out and I finished my story. "Now, I was out of it at this point, so the rest of my story is pure speculation. I imagine he undressed me with this hand," I said before repeating the process on his other hand. Just like before, he screamed until he blacked out. "Then, I imagine he used this to penetrate me and take my virginity." I grabbed the machete and pointed at his dick with it. I noticed a few more of who I assumed were my father's men make their exit. "Now, I could have gotten Sunjai to get me a brand spanking new machete, but I'm positive the process of raping me wasn't easy, so I didn't want this easy either. There was ripping and tearing, so he will get ripping and tearing," I said as I lifted the knife and, after four swings, separated his dick from his body. I didn't know if he was dead at this point or the pain cause him to black out once again, and I didn't care either. "And for my final trick, he used this mouth to call Breeze and Noelle his daughters," I said, grabbing a gun and emptying the clip into his head, as it exploded like a watermelon. I spun around and saw tears in the eyes of Blessing, Sunjai, and Sincere.

"Sinaya, I had no idea-" Sincere started.

"Nah, don't cry for me, I'm good. After this, we can talk; I owe you that for saving my kids."

"What are we doing with this one?" Sunjai asked, pointing to an unconscious Snake.

"Oh, that one is on Ghost; that was his friend. I'm ready to shower and cuddle with my girls," I said, stepping back.

"Oh, you finally done now? Since you carrying on like you ain't pregnant and shit!" Ghost snapped. I knew the real reason he was pissed off was because of the story I just told about Ahmad. I had never gone into detail before. "You been running this show, so do you." Rolling my eyes, I shrugged then lifted my gun and sent a bullet through the middle of Snake's eyes.

"Burn them and everything in the building," I said to the rest of Sincere's crew that was standing around. I needed to lay eyes on my babies.

Chapter 22

Celeste

"Are you nervous?" Sincere asked for the tenth time.

"You have no idea. I've waited for this moment forever and here it is, and I don't know what to tell them," I confessed. After the events that unfolded in Louisiana, Sin and Blessing decided we could meet and talk, and they were now on the way to the house.

"Will Young be here?"

"No, he's dealing with Aimee's burial; I wish he would let me help out or something, but he refuses." I was worried about Young; he said he was fine and hid it well that he was hurting, but a mother always knows. My thoughts were interrupted by the ringing of the doorbell. I knew it had to be Sinaya and Blessing because the guards let them in without calling. Swinging the door open, I smiled as all three of my daughters walked in. I was beyond excited that they formed the close knit bond they had, despite their feelings towards Sincere and I.

"Hey ma, where's dad?" Sunjai asked, kissing me on the cheek.

"Should be coming down in a moment, I have no idea if your brother will be coming," I said, looking at my watch.

"No, he isn't; we just left from by him. He said after the morning he had, he just wanted to be alone. We have Aimee's funeral planned out and paid for though. Get this, Sinaya volunteered to read!" I couldn't say I wasn't shocked because I could have sworn Sin hated her.

"I didn't hate the girl, but she did die behind my drama," she said, sitting down on the bar stool closest to her.

"Speaking of which, how is Rock?" I asked, genuinely concerned.

"He's doing a lot better. The rehab is really helping, along with the help of a certain dark skinned cutie who has been visiting him," she said, eyeing Sunjai. I couldn't say I was surprised. Sunjai lived to help people. "Anyway, let's talk. I didn't come here to hear why you left because I've heard enough about that. I've spent so much time being angry at you for leaving when I was a child that I couldn't appreciate your presence now," she started as Sincere made his appearance. "I appreciate the hell out of ya'll for coming back because you didn't have to. I will say, this isn't going to instantly be a Brady Bunch family, but I know Blessing wants an opportunity to have a bond with you and I can't be the reason she doesn't."

"So, Blessing is the only reason you came today?" Sincere asked with hurt in his voice.

"That and the fact that my daughters keep asking about the nice lady they met. You could have told them who you were to them. I'm fine with that. I can't say that I will come around as fast as everyone else, but I will try to give it an honest effort. I'm still so mad with the way everything played out. Blessing made me leave all of my guns in the car, in case I snapped, but I'm good. I haven't had to say my chant either time one of you spoke, so we're making progress." She laughed.

"I can respect that. Blessing, you are really quiet?"

"I'm just saying a prayer that she doesn't flip cause I know she keep a gun on her somewhere." She laughed. "But, no, I welcome the opportunity also. I've wanted to for a while, but what my sister says goes. She's been here for me from day one so, if she decided not to meet, neither was I."

"That's that loyalty; Young and I are the same damn way," Sunjai said, causing me to nod. "Ma, what are you crying for?" I wiped a tear I didn't realize was there. My prayers were answered and this was all I ever wanted.

Chapter 23

Rello

I looked at the card in my hand and made the call that I had been dreading, but it was necessary. I never thought I would be willingly calling a detective or any cop, for that matter. After a thirty-minute phone call and setting up a time to stop in, I thought about what led me to this decision.

Sin: I found my kids and I'm hopping on a plane now to get them. The crew is with me, you're in charge.

Me: I got it, be careful ma. Protect my seed.

I was hoping Ghost saw my text; I know I pissed his ass off every time I called the baby my seed, so that's why I kept doing it. A nigga be bored and, every time he gets mad, I get at least seven chuckles from his wanna be hulk ass. I hopped up; I quickly showered, then threw on a black Polo v-neck, a pair of light wash Levis, and a pair of Gamma Blue 11's. I chose to push my old school Monte Carlo today as I cruised the streets. After making a few stops, I headed to the warehouse to chop it up with the team that was left behind. We got the shipment for that night, planned it out, and then everyone went their separate ways. I was on the way home when I noticed a cop following close behind me. I damn sure wasn't bringing them to my home and I had seen too many cops that were trigger happy, so I wasn't stopping my black ass on this deserted street. Knowing I had warrants, I drove my ass straight to the police department. Imagine my surprise when they hauled me in and threw pictures of Sin, Ghost, Streetz, and Blessing on the table. I did what I had to do, then got the fuck outta there.

Pulling up at the warehouse, I looked at all the cars parked here for the meeting. I called then grabbed the manila folder and hopped out. Walking in, I didn't miss Streetz and Ghost mugging me, so I flashed them my grills, then blew a kiss to Sin. Fuck them!

"Get fucked up behind my wife, pussy!" Ghost snapped.

"Oh, my bad son, I didn't see a ring. And last time I checked, she was single. As a matter of fact, I wasn't even blowing a kiss to Sin; that was for my seed. You just make sure your ass don't be rubbing on her stomach and shit; that's disrespectful to the real daddy," I said, smiling even wider when he got up from his seat.

"Rello, you called us here for a reason, wassup?" Sin asked. I paused for a moment and smiled at the way her skin was glowing. The all-black jumpsuit she was wearing did little to hid her baby bump; looking down at her feet, I shook my head.

"Is your ass supposed to be wearing those shoes?" I asked, knowing it would piss off Ghost.

"Nigga, that ain't got shit to do with you; find your ass some business and stop worrying about mine," he spat as Streetz held him back.

"Well fuck, half of her is my business; fuck you mean? Those shoes can't be comfortable while she carrying my seed nigga! If she fall, pussy, you better catch her," I said back, grilling him. Fuck it, I wouldn't be working for them after today anyway. "And

Streetz, you can let him go cause there ain't no hoe in my blood. That nigga bleed like I bleed; what the fuck!"

"I didn't come here to hear about Sin feet or to hear you two go back and forth. Speak ya'll piece, so I can dip. In case ya'll forgot, I have a very handsome son waiting up for me and I'd much rather be cuddled up with him," Blessing said, walking in behind me. I laughed as she walked over and sat on Streetz's lap. Her and her sister was really those bitches you only read about in those urban books.

"Aye, keep your eyes off mine nigga; behind this one, I'll body your whole family," Streetz said, causing me to laugh harder.

"All due respect Blessing but, Streetz, don't nobody but your ass wanna sleep with one eye open if you forget to take out the trash one night. Anyway, this meeting was more so a farewell party for ya boy," I said, placing the folder in front of Sin. I watched as her face frowned up from the various pictures of her that spanned over a year.

"What the fuck is this?" she said, handing the pictures to Blessing.

"I was pulled over by a detective who was very interested in you. From what I learned, Snake started snitching on Ghost and Streetz before he died. The day ya'll went out there, he had a phone interview with the detective that he missed. I'll assume he was tied up when they called him. Anyway, he never gave any information on Sin and Blessing, just Ghost and Streetz. They tried finding information on those two but found out ya'll were the heads of the organization. The charges you were all brought up on was enough to lock you up for the rest of your life, but all they had was Snake's word and they were hoping mine. I told them I would help initially, but only so I could leave and come let you know. When I called them before coming here, they asked for names, so I told them mine. I know they only had the fact that I had warrants and they found some weed in my car. So, I'll be turning myself in tomorrow morning," I finished.

"What the fuck?" Sin stood up quickly and started rubbing her belly. The look of anger in her eyes quickly turned into amusement. "Oh, the baby just kicked!" she said, looking between Ghost and I. Blessing jumped up to feel on her stomach, as Ghost stared me down. I burst out laughing and decided to stop fucking with them.

"Nigga, feel your child kick and stop watching me." I laughed as all eyes fell on me.

"What you mean; you think going to jail relieves you of your duties? Ya'll will still be taking a DNA test," Blessing snapped.

"I mean, we can, but there is no need. I was in an accident when I was younger; there will be no kids coming from Rello." I burst out laughing again. "I been wanting to tell ya'll, but fucking with Ghost was too good to pass by. Sin, yo ass not the only one with anger problems ma."

"This nigga!" I heard Murda and Gutta say at the same time, as Blessing and Streetz fell out laughing.

"So, if the cop wouldn't have stopped you, how long would you carry this shit on?" Blessing asked, still laughing.

"Shit, I was goin be smiling in the delivery room like a proud father," I said with a serious face cause that really was my plans. "Nah but, on the real, I'm out; I need to get my mans wet before he be on a lockdown." I laughed, heading for the door.

"Rello, you know I got you while you're down right?" Sin asked.

"Yeah ma, you more solid than niggas I grew up with. I'll hit you up later baby mama; I gotta see you before I go," I said before looking at Ghost. "And a nigga ain't on that shit so be cool." I walked out, hearing him chuckle behind my back. I had one thought on my mind and that was to roll up on Sasha's freaky ass.

Chapter 24

Ghost

No one had to tell me a nigga already knew he fucked up. That shit at the warehouse wasn't supposed to go like that, but Sin took a nigga there. I didn't mean any of the shit I said; fuck, I knew Sin wasn't a hoe, but for this nigga to really be laughing about fucking my bitch had me on ten. I initially wanted to kill both of their asses for playing with me; fuck, I still wanted to kill Rello's bitch ass.

I couldn't say that Rello dropping that bomb on me didn't make me the happiest man alive. I had already decided that I wouldn't push the issue of a DNA test until Sin said something, but now there was no need and I could move forward with what I had in mind. I was getting my girl back, tonight! I would owe Rello my life for that charge he took for Sin. I respected that he told me he loved her enough to let her go, but I wouldn't trust his ass alone with her. Even after he told me that shit, he hit her ass with a smile that had her trying hard not to smile back and I damn sure didn't like that shit.

Me: Hey can I come see my kids tonight please?

Wifey: Sure if you want to take her with you for the night. I'll have Breeze's bag packed.

Me: Just coming visit, my new house isn't ready yet, and what do you mean Breeze? I want to see both of my kids.

Wifey: Oh, now they're both yours. Call before you come.

I didn't bother to reply because I damn sure didn't want to start an argument. I had an idea, but a nigga was nervous on if I could pull it off or not so, after making a few stops, I went see the one person that could help, Blessing.

"Wassup Streetz, Beretta here?" I asked once Streetz opened the door.

"Yeah, but I don't think you want to talk to her, son; she ain't even fucking with you anymore and she not even trying to hide it. You know how my girl is." He laughed. I already knew, after that episode at the warehouse, she would have felt some way about me but a nigga was more desperate than a lil bit.

"Shit, I know; that's why I wore my bulletproof vest," I told him, dead ass serious. I knew Red spared me out of love; Blessing didn't love a nigga like that.

"That shit won't help you one bit because I'm delivering all headshots anyway. The fuck you want with me, Ghost?" Blessing whispered, coming from the back of the house carrying a sleeping Eli.

"I come in peace; I need your help though, on some real shit," I said, sounding as desperate as I was.

"I did help you; you walked out that warehouse with your life after disrespecting my sister. Shit, you walked out after putting your hands on my sister. I helped you a lot. You can thank Breeze for that though; I figured at least one of her biological parents could stay in

164

her life," she said and I believed her because she stared me in the eyes without a smile or even a smirk in sight.

"Man, I know I fucked up, but I need your help..." After an hour of begging, I finally got her on my side and she planned the night that would help me get Red back.

***

"I'm goin kill Streetz and Blessing," Sin said as she walked into her house. I had Blessing and Streetz tell her I could go see the girls at their house, since she didn't want to be bothered with me. While she was there dropping off the kids, I came over and set up the dinner I picked up, courtesy of her favorite spot, Red Lobster, then placed roses and candles around the dining room area. A nigga was more nervous than a lil bit, but I knew Red wasn't going to hold the last few weeks against me.

"We never really talked after everything happened Red."

"Why do you find the need to speak to a hoe? Isn't that what you called me?" she asked in a dry tone.

"Man, we both said some things we didn't mean. How many times did you call me pussy?" I asked.

"No, you said things you didn't mean. I meant every single word that came from my mouth when I said it. You claim to be a different breed of nigga, but you're just the same as the rest. You niggas don't know how to take a woman giving you a dosage of your own medicine," she spat.

"I didn't come here to argue Sin. I'm here to talk, nothing more nothing less. I miss you, and I need you and my kids back." I laid it on the line. What I didn't expect was for her to start laughing like I was Cedric the entertainer or Bernie Mac.

"So, Rello lets you know that it can't be his child and, all of a sudden, you need us back? What if I say Rello wasn't the only possible, then what?" she asked, making me instantly see red.

"You was fucking someone else Red?" I asked as calm as I possibly could.

"No but, from your reaction, I can imagine if I was, then you damn sure wouldn't be this same man standing in front of me. Ghost, get out my house but leave the food."

"How you kick a nigga out but want the shit I bought?" I laughed at her nerve.

"Shit because your child is hungry; just cause you were a horrible boyfriend doesn't mean you have to be a horrible father." She laughed.

"That shit ain't funny; I don't play behind my kids. Besides, I ain't really asking to be your boyfriend anymore Red. That shit wasn't working for me no way," I said as her beautiful face turned up into a deadly mug.

"Then, what the fuck you came to my shit for? You broke in, lit these stank ass candles, and dropped all these cheap ass rose petals to say that? Yo ass could have said that from the jump, but

166

you decide to cheat on me with that nappy headed hoe and get her pregnant," she started going off.

"Red, chill bruh, I ain't mean that shit like that. You took it wrong maw. A nigga cheating wasn't on you at all; that was all on my dumb ass. I fucked up, but I ain't going down that road ever again." I quickly calmed her down before shit went left.

"So, what way did you mean it?"

"I meant being just your boyfriend ain't enough for me any more ma." I pulled the light blue ring box from my pocket and got down on one knee.

"Sin, I love you more than I can put in words. Life without you means nothing to me. You make everything right in my life. You've blessed me with the family I've always dreamed of. You look out for me more than anyone else has ever looked out for me. Hell, you look out for me more than I look out for myself. I have never in my life prayed for anyone more than I pray for you. You've been through so much hurt in your life and it kills me to know that I added to that hurt, instead of subtracting from it. To be real, I could go on for hours with the apologies that I know I owe you and that still wouldn't be enough time. So, give me forever to apologize and make up for all that I put you through. Let me be the one to make sure the only tears you cry are of joy or from my big headed child being born. Sin, I swear, I'll never hurt you again. Will you marry me?"

Chapter 25

Sinaya

Rello letting me know he couldn't have children really took a load off of my shoulder. I was sure it was probably too late to realize, but I knew I couldn't see myself with him in the long run anyway. He was a friend when I needed one and kept my mind off of Ghost when I needed him for that too. And, of course, he was there for that other thing also. Rello going away for my shit showed me what kind of man he was and I would forever look out for him because of it. Thinking back to our conversation, I knew that I would forever love him, just not in that way, and I was glad I could keep him in my life.

"You know I got you through whatever, right?" I asked him *as I dropped him off to turn himself in.*

"Shit, I just need you to pull those strings and get a nigga the least amount of time possible."

"How long did they say they were offering?"

"Shit, I told my lawyer don't even fucking tell me. I knew you could get whatever it was they offered me reduced. But, on some real shit, if a nigga heard numbers that sounded too damn long, you was gone to jail son." He laughed

"I'm going take care of it for you. You have my word."

"I don't doubt that but, while you taking care of everything, who is going to take care of you? And don't think I'm coming on to

yo funky ass cause I been there and done that. But, for real ma, you can't run from your problems. Stop being so damn mean all the time and deal with your shit. When Ghost did all that shit, your first thought was to run, and you ain't even that type of female. I'm going against the grain telling you this but, as a nigga, he goin fuck up. And fix your face cause I ain't saying that you're supposed to accept anything from him. But if that's where you wanna be, which I know it is, then you will have to accept that he fucked up just like you did. Now, don't get me wrong; a nigga is happy as fuck you chose to run off on his ass and come to daddy, but that ain't you, ma. Work on Sinaya and stop trying to be everything for everyone. That ain't your job. You are only obligated to be there for your children, ma."

"Thank you, Rello; if nothing else, you'll always have me as a friend, regardless of what my relationship status is," I said, wiping away a tear.

"So what, you not taking him back?"

"I don't know, why?" I asked after seeing him smile.

"Cause shit, if not, a nigga wanna know if you goin sneak me some pictures when you write me? Or when I get my cellphone, you goin snapchat me that pussy, if it's cool?" he asked laughing.

"Boy, get yo ass out my car." I laughed

"Nah but, for real, come see a nigga from time to time. Tell Ghost I won't even have to wrap up when they give us conjugal visits," he said before leaning over and kissing me on the mouth. "I love yo ass Sin."

"I love you too, Rello."

And here I sat on stuck because everything he said made sense, and I never saw it until it was pointed out. I spent every day of my life making sure everyone else was good and never really got to know myself. It was draining being everything for everyone, but I handled it because it really and truly kept my mind off of my own problems. I was deep in thought until I got a text from my biggest problem to date.

Breeze's father: Hey, can I come see my kids tonight please?

I knew that I couldn't keep him away from Breeze because biologically, I had no say so when it came to her. I had been petty the past few days because I damn sure hadn't been allowing him to be near her. I didn't say that to say I wasn't petty anymore so, of course, I thought on my answer.

Me: Sure if you want to take her with you for the night, I'll have Breeze's bag packed.

I laughed sending that text off but, fuck it, he made sure he said just Breeze was his child, so we would keep it that way. It didn't take long for him to respond back.

Breeze's Father: Just coming visit, my new house isn't ready yet, and what do you mean Breeze. I want to see both of my kids.

The new house was news to me but after the mess Peaches left behind there, I don't blame him.

Me: Oh, now they're both yours. Call before you come.

I didn't have any plans or anything of that nature to do but, of course, his ass didn't need to know that. He was no longer my man, so we damn sure wasn't having pop up visits. I must have dozed off because I woke up to Blessing calling. After telling her how much I didn't want to see Ghost, she came up with the best plan ever, so here I was dropping off the kids.

"You look cute; do you have plans?" she asked, making me look down at my attire. I had gotten dressed earlier before going pick up Rello from his home. It was a simple denim jumpsuit that hid my growing bump and I threw on a pair of snakeskin Jimmy Choo's.

"What, this old thing?" I asked, spinning around as I gave her the girls' bag. She offered to have them sleep over so more power to them. "No, I'm going home and Netflix and chill by my damn self, since you're kidnapping my girls." I laughed.

"Well, you need the break; besides, you never know what the night brings," she added smiling.

"Ma, you staying sleep with us?" Breeze asked. She had been calling me ma for like a month now and, although at first I was uncomfortable about it, it had grown on me.

"No baby, this is for cool girls only; ma just goin try to stop us from eating sweets all night," Blessing loudly whispered in her ear.

"Oh yeah ma, sorry, but you can't stay. Nanny B said we don't have any more room," she lied.

"Oh ok, I see how it is. I'm leaving anyway. And you and Streetz don't be doing anything freaky with my babies here hoe," I whispered in Blessing's ear before walking to my car and heading home. The radio definitely wasn't on my side, as Tamar Braxton was singing about heading home to her man. I quickly turned it off and got lost in my thoughts for the rest of the ride because the only thing I was heading home to was my dogs. Pulling into my garage, I noticed the light that I normally left on in the kitchen was turned off, so I immediately grabbed my gun. I smelled him before I saw him and, when I finally did lay eyes on him, I was pleasantly surprised. Ghost definitely had been looking rough lately, so to see him dressed up with a fresh lining and retwist did something to me. I wanted to immediately kick him out, but I smelled the cheddar bay biscuits and my mouth started to water. He knew exactly what he was doing. Everyone knew I was addicted to those and this pregnancy wasn't helping any, so I heard him out. What I didn't expect was the proposal at the end of it all. I knew I loved Ghost beyond what any human being was capable of loving another, but I didn't know if it was enough. Wiping the tears from my eyes, I backed away from where he was kneeling with his ring.

"Ghost, I love you more than I could put in words, but I can't marry you. Not right now anyway," I said and was instantly heartbroken when I saw the pain flash in his eyes.

"What you mean you can't marry me right now Red? As in if I come back tomorrow and do this shit again, you'll say yeah or as in you just sparing a nigga so you don't want to say you'll never be with me again?" he asked with hurt lacing his voice.

"Ghost, I don't know what you want me to say. I need to find what works for me and it's painfully obvious that this isn't it right now. You hurt me in more ways than I care to count and you could possibly say the same. Shit ain't working between us and I can't be happy with you if I'm not happy with me right now. I almost failed my kids because I was too busy playing get back at you. Sleeping with Rello before I ended things with you was some disloyal shit and I've never been disloyal. I let someone I loved knock me off my square and I never want that to happen again. I put you above myself and above my kids and, in return, that led to them being taken from me. I used to be all about Noelle before I met you; no one would have ever gotten that close to her. I owe her and Breeze to be that woman again. What would have happened if we didn't get to them in time? I sleep with them every night because I fear them being taken from me. I have plans on sneaking back to Blessing's house because I can't stand being away from them. I have to focus on them for once."

"I respect that Red. I don't like it, but I respect the shit outta what you saying. I'm not giving up on you though, ma. I'm goin let you do you and be here for my kids in the meantime. As soon as you figure out what you need to figure out, I'll be right back on bended knee," he said before kissing my cheek and walking out the door. There was a chance I just pushed him into the arms of another woman and that was a chance I was willing to take for my sanity.

Epilogue

3 years later

Sinaya

Tears filled my eyes as I stared myself over in the mirror and I was trying my hardest not to mess up my makeup. To say I was against this whole setup, Sunjai and Blessing surely exceeded any expectation I may have had. From the elegant blush colored strapless Pnina Tornai gown I was wearing, down to the nude colored Louboutin heels that Blessing insisted I wear, every single detail came together perfectly on my wedding day. After leaving Ghost, I never thought I would be getting married. I didn't think I would ever love so deeply again. But God sure has a sense of humor. If I thought I would be able to stop myself from crying, my children walking in surely canceled those plans. Breeze and Noelle looked so beautiful in their matching flower girl dresses with the flat replica of my heels, but they didn't even take the cake; it was Eli and Noah who came in wearing their little white and black tuxedos that really pulled at my heart strings. When I looked up and saw my father, Sincere, I knew it was show time.

Here we are, together

And everything between us is good

I'm right here in this cloud, baby

Ready to fly but before I take

Another step

Would you catch me if I fall for you?

'Cause I'm falling

I'm falling, I'm falling

I'm so used to standing

So used to being on my own

But this thing is new, baby

It feels like I'm losing control

I'll take another step

If you catch me when I fall for you

'Cause I'm falling

I'm falling, I'm falling

Will you promise to be there?

Stay by my side always?

Whenever I need you

Don't let me down, no, no

The tears ran down my face uncontrollably as Leela James stood in front of the church singing my song, our song. If you would have told me three years ago I would have been here, I would have laughed in your face. Through all the shit we've been through over the years, who knew I would find my way back to Ghost? When I turned down his proposal, I was uncertain on what the future held for us. What I did know was without a shadow of a doubt, he would take care of his responsibility because he was and would always be a great father. For the first year, we did really well co-parenting. We even started seeing other people, but that didn't last too long. I guess the guy I was dating was scared of Ghost's reputation and ran off. For some reason or the other, Ghost blamed me for his failed relationship, although I was on my best behavior.

I looked up just in time to see Ghost wiping tears from his eyes and had to squeeze my legs together because that nigga had me dripping in church. I didn't care who caught my attention over the years; they never had me like Ghost had me. That's why I was sitting here about to pop from the weight of these damn twins I was carrying. That's right; Ghost had got me again, good this time. A drunken night at Streetz and Blessing's wedding led to us being in a hotel room going at it until room service came knocking the next morning. I kissed my father, then my mother on the cheek, and made my way to my man. The pastor was speaking, but I was too busy mouthing what I would do to him when I got him back in the room. Feeling Blessing nudge me in the back and hearing the laughter around us, I knew that it was my time to say my vows. Handing my bouquet to Sunjai, I began:

"I sat down and wrote this whole sheet worth of words on how I was going to love, honor, and obey, but it just came out not being me. So, I chose to scrap that idea and speak from my heart.

176

Deion, I don't know how I made it through my life without you in it. Before you, it was only Noelle and I, and I thought that I was satisfied with my life, but in you walked and you gave me substance. You and Breeze came and, just when I thought our family was complete, you helped to truly complete our circle with Eli, then Jour'nai and Ja'nai. I can't thank you enough for making me the woman I am today. I was so angry at the world and no one could handle me until you. You let me know it was okay to be soft, trusting, and to just be a woman. You let me know that I didn't need to handle every single detail and that you could help carry the load. You are more than my fiancé; you are my best friend, my soulmate, my shelter from the rain, and my calm in all storms. So, on today, I vow to be the best mother and role model to our kids, to remain by your side whether good or bad times, to being your cheerleader whether you are on or off your game, and above all, follow your lead because it has never steered me wrong. It's always been you and it will always be you that I choose. I loved you then, I love you now, and I will always love you, Ghost."

Ghost

A nigga was getting married and I'd be damned if I didn't say I was nervous. If I knew it was anyone other than Sin meeting me in front of all these people, I would have left this church about an hour ago. It took us a while to get to this point after she decided to walk away from me. I'm still trying to understand what she meant when she needed time to see where she wanted to be. Sinaya had to know I wasn't letting her be happy with anyone other than me. I knew I put her through a lot of shit but, like any man, I felt that I deserved Sin. Despite all my fuck ups and my many flaws, God made her for only me and no one else could love her better than I could. And a nigga wasn't trying to see if she could find better anyway. In the year and a half that we were just co-parenting, I had a female to occupy my time, thinking it would make Sin wake the fuck up. But what did she do? Start dating pussy ass Daniel again. Where the fuck did this nigga keep popping up from? And what hold did he have on my bitch to keep her running back? Shit, that ain't my concern anymore; he ain't really anyone's concern anymore. Sin thought he just ran off and I'd let her think that. Just like I let her ass think I didn't know what her, Blessing, and Sunjai did to Lena, the chick I was messing with.

Even after that, she wasn't really fucking with me, talking about some I had to date her again. Sinaya really had me staying in a separate house and coming over for date nights, then going home with nothing but a kiss here and there. Then, she was talking about tying her tubes cause she was done with kids. My children are my life and I wanted more; plus, I knew that would be my key to getting back in the house. My plan was to get her knocked up, so I could come back home to my family. Then, when we finally started fucking again, I could only have sex with her if I was wearing a condom. How the fuck was I going get her pregnant again strapping up? Desperate times called for desperate measures. I waited for my opportunity, Blessing and Streetz's wedding, then kept giving her ass shots while I was taking shots of H2O. Long story short, I struck gold.

Now, here I was staring at the most beautiful creature God could ever create and wondering how I almost lost her. Sin wasn't an emotional person, even while pregnant, so her crying right now was something I wasn't used to, but it let me know those words were from the heart; how do I top that?

"How am I supposed to go after those vows? Anything I say will sound mediocre, but I'll try. Sinaya, you have to know that God made you for me and me only. You're my equal in every form of the word. Where I'm lacking, you right there to pick up the slack. I knew there was no one else for me when you took my daughter as your own; you never treated her any differently than our other kids. I fell in love with you right around the same time Breeze did. No, we haven't had this perfect relationship, but I know, beyond a shadow of a doubt, there is no one out there that will love you better or stronger. You were made with me in mind, with all of my likes and needs from a woman taken into consideration. I vow to love you and our kids past my last breath, respect you, and hold you above all else for the rest of my days. I love you, Red."

Blessing

Watching Sinaya and Ghost share their first dance made my mind drift back to my wedding day. To think I wouldn't give Streetz the time of day, we are so madly in love with each other. That man balances me off so much, it is crazy. I've retired from my illegal activity, all except for helping out Sin. Streetz told me he wasn't carrying out contracts anymore, but I knew better. That was fine though because he obviously needed something to occupy his time;

any time he could kill someone he was happy. Last week, Noah said his teacher, Mr. Robert, hit him and that night he was found dead. I knew it was no one but Streetz's extra ass. Everyone knows that Noah exaggerates. If I tell him no to something, he says I hit him, and I know for a fact Mr. Robert's old ass knew what I was capable of, so he would never touch him. But that's my husband for you. Everything with my parents was behind us. After we finally had a sit down, we never brought up the past again and just worked on what was to come. I missed Annette dearly; despite her past, she was the only mother I knew for a while and the fact that I would never see her again hurts. I could only pray she took care of Neema up there. Who thought that crazy ass Blessing would finally find love and have a family of her own? Not me. Thank ya'll for coming on this crazy ride, until next time…

Streetz

It was my nigga's wedding and I couldn't even turn up like I wanted to. I was too busy watching Blessing's ass. I made sure I kept my eye on Blessing every time she attempted to walk to that bar. Although I loved the fuck out of my wife, I wasn't just watching her because she was fine. She can keep acting like Sin the only one carrying a load if she wanted to. I'm hoping it's my girl; I'm not trying to replace Neema, but I can't handle another Noah. That lil nigga bad as fuck; he walk around terrorizing shit. Last week, he made me kill an innocent man. He told me his teacher hit him then, after I handled him, the next morning, his lil ass looks at me and said, "I lied yesterday. Mr. Robert didn't hit me; I just wanted him to let me color." I would have whipped his lil ass, but Blessing be trying to fight a nigga for hitting "her son" as she calls him like the lil nigga ain't half me. Ghost and Sin already banned him from the house, talking about he be having Eli in all kinds of shit. Man, if you ask me, both of their asses some lil pint size ass Chuckie's. I had not one complaint though; a nigga from the hood was married with kids and sitting on more money than my machines can count. I'm out!

Young

A nigga was out here naked without Aimee. She was all I really knew. My family has my back and this is definitely not the end of Young. You know nothing keeps a young rich nigga down for long, someone told me I would get my happily ever after real soon.

Rello

Don't count a young nigga out yet. I heard Trenae' already has Rello's story in the works, so you'll definitely be hearing from me again. Sin pulled some strings; a nigga only had to serve 4 years in here. Three years down already.

The End

Sneak Peek:

You Going Pay Me in Tears: Two Sides to Every Story

Prologue

Reign

"Royal, c'mon get up and get in the bed," I said, shaking my sister who was in her usual spot, asleep on the bathroom floor. I sure wish this morning sickness of hers would pass so that I wasn't constantly woken up out of my sleep because it decided to always hit at like four in the morning. Don't get me wrong; I'll do anything for my twin, but this started during the ending of my senior year and you know what that means, finals.

"Nah, it's way worst today sis; I'm so tired of running back and forth to the toilet, so I'll just sleep here," Royal answered without lifting her head or even opening her eyes.

"Ok, well so am I," I said, running to grab a blanket and pillow. Lying against the floor was very uncomfortable but, for my sister and my niece or nephew, I would sacrifice it; besides, it was already five in the morning. I could squeeze in another hour and a half of sleep before heading to my school for the last time in my high school career. I thought of the move I was making on Monday morning until I dozed off.

"Royal and Reign, ya'll asses bet not miss that damn bus or you'll be walking to school, and you know Reign fat ass doesn't like to walk anywhere!" Chantelle screamed through the bathroom door, waking us up later than I would have liked. The fat joke coming from her was nothing new. Chantelle was my mother, although she told us don't call her that, and she hated my soul. Jumping up after waking Royal, I ran to my room where I already had my clothes laid out for the day and thanked God I showered last night. In twenty minutes flat, I had freshened up, gotten dressed, and threw my natural hair in a high bun. Walking into my sister's room, I smiled at her because the baby really had her glowing. We shared the same face and complexion, but that was where it ended. My sister was very active in sports, while I focused strictly on my studies. She really could have been the next Flo Jo; she was that amazing and her body definitely showed. Even with the bulge in her belly, Royal could give Teyana Taylor a run for her money body wise. While I, on the other hand, was more of Jill Scott's size and was perfectly happy with my curves. I guess I was supposed to be ashamed of them, according to my mother, but I wasn't. In fact, I flaunted those bad boys; like today, I was wearing a red, loose fitted crop top that said 'thug life', a pair of white, high waisted jean jeggings and some all black chucks with a red black and white plaid shirt wrapped around my waist. Normally, I wouldn't show much skin because I wouldn't want to cause problems with my teachers but, being that it's the last day, this would be the least of their worries.

"You're looking cute." My sister nodded her head at my attire.

"So are you." I admired the basketball jersey she wore as a dress, with a pair of chucks also. "Sis, I have a question; when did you know you were ready to have sex?"

"Shit, I wasn't, to be honest; my child's father asked and I was too scared to say no. Why, you aren't thinking of giving Troy no ass, right?" She put me on front street.

"Well, he has been patient; we've been dating for two years. Plus, with me going away for school, I don't need him looking for options elsewhere. You don't think I should? I'm sure he's getting bored with just head and sticking the tip in." I noticed Royal rolling her eyes and knew she was gonna let me have it. Her and Troy hated each other and were forever arguing.

"I'll tell you like this; a baby isn't even keeping these niggas, so what you think sex going to do? A nigga will cheat with you in the next room if the opportunity presents itself. Keep your head in the books and get outta here before you're trapped like me," she said, wiping a lonely tear that dropped. I knew she was thinking of her baby's father that wanted nothing to do with her or the kid.

"Um, let's go catch the bus," I said, grabbing my purse. The walk to the bus stop and the ride to school was quiet, as we were both wrapped in our own thoughts. My mind was on the sex; I already knew I was having with Troy. I knew I loved him and never had a problem with females saying he cheated in the two years we had dated, so that had to count for something, right? I was so wrapped up in my thoughts, I didn't realize we were already pulling up at school. Climbing off the bus, I headed to homeroom, where we were handed our cap and gowns. I wasn't excited as my peers because I wasn't attending graduation anyway; besides Royal and Troy, I had no family to celebrate with. I already knew my mother wasn't coming and she was the only family I had. Plus, I was heading to the college early to begin work study and help Royal with some of the baby's expenses. The bell ringing pulled me from my daze and I headed out, bumping right into Troy.

"Wassup ma, where you rushing to like that?" he asked, licking his lips. I looked him over and smiled; Troy was on his way to being the captain of the football team and had the arrogance that came along with it. He was 6'4" with the body of a God, high yellow with green eyes that were to die for. His only flaw was that grill, Lord. If he didn't smile, he was perfect, but don't crack at joke because he looked like a piranha by the mouth. Of course, I'd never say it out loud because that was my baby. Just like my sister, he was gonna be here another year because I was graduating early.

"Nothing, heading to English, I think I may ditch P.E.; where will you be then? That's the last class I have to go to and I'm thinking we can ditch after that."

"Word," he said, brushing his head full of waves," what you trying to do like that?" he asked.

"Your mama at work today, right?" I asked, noticing Royal heading our way.

"Yeah, oh shit, you really wanna go through with what you said last night?" he asked, putting two and two together.

"Yep!" I popped the p. "So, don't have me waiting forever."

"Shit, if you serious, I'm leaving now. Just call me when you're on the way ma," he said with a huge smile on his face.

I walked off to meet Royal, who stood a distance away while mugging the hell out of Troy.

"I don't know why you deal with alligator mouth," she said. I ignored her as we walked to our next class, which was next door to each other. After hearing the speeches about how the world was ours and being dismissed early, I decided to head to the P.E. building to freshen up. I laughed to myself as I fished my feminine wipes from my locker, as Betty Wright's song, *Tonight is the Night*, played through my head.

"I'm nervous and I'm trembling'

Waiting for you to walk in

I'm trying hard to relax

But I just can't keep still, no"

My singing was interrupted when I heard my sister crying and pleading on the phone to her baby's father. I heard her begging him all the time to be in their life but, from what she told me, he was in a relationship and told her to abort the child. She swears she didn't know he was in a relationship, but I think she's lying.

"I don't get why it's so hard to understand that I love you; we have created something beautiful and you're willing to just throw it away. I'm tired of begging you to see that with me is where you should be. You better fucking leave her, or I'll tell her and she'll leave you. Either way, I fucking win." I really wanted to snatch the phone from her hands. She was too gorgeous to beg any man for anything. I walked over to do just that when he hung up in her face. "Hello... hello? I know the fuck he didn't," she said, noticing me standing there. "I'm glad you decided not to ditch; let me go deal with my sorry ass excuse of a baby daddy, and I'll meet you back here before your class gets over," she told me, quickly wiping her tears. I didn't even have the chance to tell her that I was still skipping because she was gone as soon as those words left her lips.

Heading into a stall, I used my feminine wipes, then switched out of my boy shorts into the lace thong that matched the bra set I was wearing. Making sure I didn't miss any body part, I lotioned myself down with Bath and Body Works, Mad About You, that Troy seemed to love, then redressed in the clothes I wore to school. Walking over to the mirror, I shook my head at my bun that was once cute. Grabbing my purse, I whipped out a brush and wet it under the faucet to brush my hair back, then lathered my lips with a layer of MAC's boy bait. Blowing myself a kiss, I knew I was going to really shock Troy; I had been watching old pornos of my girl Pinky and couldn't wait to get past the boring part of losing my virginity, so I could show him the tricks I have been practicing. I had even practiced my oral skills on a banana and a cucumber and could damn near swallow them whole without gagging; I loved doing it, so he was in for a treat. I waited a few minutes for the bell to ring so that I could blend in with all the students moving around.

RING! RING!

My heart seemed to jump out of my chest once I finally heard it. There was no turning back; like Betty Wright said, 'he was gonna make me a woman today'. Plugging in my phone, I listened to Ciara's *Body Party,* as I made the walk to Troy's house. I was rehearsing the dance moves I made up in my head, so I wouldn't mess up once I got there. I was going for sexy and didn't need to screw it up. Walking up the steps, I started to knock but, the door was already slightly opened, and I heard Troy on the phone arguing. Shaking my head, I hoped like hell this didn't mess up our plans because he had an attitude out of this world once someone pissed him off. My thoughts were interrupted when I heard his conversation.

"Bitch, I wish the fuck you would. You knew what this was when we fucked, and you lied and said you were on birth control. I told you get rid of that child." I heard him say and my heart started pounding, as I tiptoed up the stairs towards his bedroom.

"Troy, please, I was a virgin; the fuck would I need birth control for? Don't think I didn't know what ya'll were gonna do during P.E period neither. I won't hesitate to tell her you fucked me again, just a moment ago. I don't understand why you need her anyway; fuck, we are basically the same person. I'm just a whole lot sexier." I heard my sister say, instantly breaking my heart word by word. I fell to the floor as silent tears fell from my eyes. My sister was pregnant by my boyfriend and here I was about to help raise her bastard child. I was confused; they hated each other, didn't they?

"Royal, you know what I'm capable of, play pussy and get fucked. Once she leaves for school, I can come around more; you know your mom doesn't care. But don't throw this on me; hell, you let me fuck with her in the next room. The way I see it, we both fucked up. Give daddy a kiss, so you can bounce before she comes." I heard her kiss him, then the footsteps followed; I stood to my feet, just as they turned the corner.

"You better wear a fucking condom with her," Royal said, clearly not seeing me.

"Fuck man, Reign..." Troy started, once he noticed me and he began rubbing his head, something he did when he was nervous.

"Really Troy, my fucking sister!" I cried hysterically. "Out of every bitch in this school, you picked my twin sister son!"

"Reign, calm down; you know how you get when you're upset." Royal tried to calm me down before the inevitable happened.

"And you, Royal, after everything I do for you." I cried and felt the change happening. Royal must have noticed I was too calm all of a sudden because she attempted to make Troy take a step back. At the young age of eight, I was diagnosed with dissociative identity disorder, or split personalities. Anytime something got too complicated for me, Ivy would appear and normally leave me in a world of trouble. Royal was the only person who could make her go away, but I wasn't too sure this time.

Ivy

"Ivy, you know you can't be out here! Mom said you would get committed if it happened again," Royal said, trying to make me bring Reign back. I always hated this bitch and her mother; they did nothing but use and abuse Reign and, to be honest, they were the reason I was created. Reign needed a break from all of their bullshit.

"Oh, that's what she said huh? Well, don't worry because I'll deal with her after I get done here; I have a career to end and a baby to get rid of," I said as Royal took off for the staircase and I gave her a little push to help her ass down. The sound of her screaming and tumbling down the stairs brought a smile to my face and I walked toward Troy, who kept backing up.

"Who the fuck is Ivy? Reign, what's wrong with your eyes? Are you fucking nuts; you pushed your sister down the stairs!"

"Do you know how much Reign loved you?" I asked, cocking my head to the side as my eyes fell on the trophy he just won a couple of days ago.

"What are you talking about? You are Reign."

"It's funny how she's the catch and here you are with that piranha mouth, acting like you're a godsend." I lifted the trophy as I walked closer towards him. "You know, she was so excited when you won this trophy. Who would have known it would be the cause of the end of your football career," I said, kicking him in the dick, which caused him to lean forward before I pushed him on his bed. He was so concerned with the pain; he never even saw when I brought the trophy down on his knee with all the strength I possessed. The loud cracking of his bone almost made me bust a nut, so I repeated the motion until I was tired of hearing his cries. Walking down the staircase, I stepped over Royal, who was sitting in a pool of her own blood. No one would mess with Reign as long as I was here.

Made in the USA
Lexington, KY
02 February 2018